How God Stopped The
PIRATES

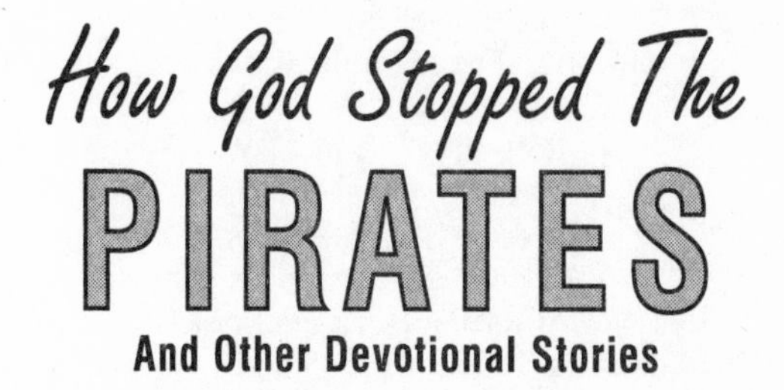

And Other Devotional Stories

Joel R. Beeke & Diana Kleyn

Illustrated by Jeff Anderson

CHRISTIAN FOCUS

Reprinted 2004 and 2005
Published by Christian Focus Publications
and Reformation Heritage Books
ISBN: 1-85792-816-4
Christian Focus Publications Ltd,
Geanies House, Fearn, Tain,
Ross-shire, IV20 1TW.
Scotland, Great Britain
www.christianfocus.com
email: info@christianfocus.com
Reformation Heritage Books
2919 Leonard St, NE, Grand Rapids, MI, 49525
Phone: 616-977-0599
Fax: 616-285-3246
email: orders@heritagebooks.org
Website: www.heritagebooks.org
Illustrations and Cover illustration by Jeff Anderson
Cover design by Alister Macinnes
Printed and bound in Denmark
by Nørhaven Paperback A/S

Building on the Rock - Book Titles and Themes
Book 1: How God Used a Thunderstorm
Living for God and The Value of Scripture
Book 2: How God Stopped the Pirates
Missionary Tales and Remarkable Conversions
Book 3: How God Used a Snowdrift
Honoring God and Dramatic Deliverances
Book 4: How God used a Drought and an Umbrella
Faithful Witnesses and Childhood Faith
Book 5: How God Sent a Dog to Save a Family
God's Care and Childhood Faith

Acknowledgements

All of the Christian stories contained in these books are based on true happenings, most of which occurred in the nineteenth century. We have gleaned them from a variety of sources, including several books by Richard Newton, then rewrote them in contemporary language. Many of them are printed here for the first time; others were previously printed, without the accompanying devotional material, in a series titled *Building on the Rock* by the Netherlands Reformed Book and Publishing and by Reformation Heritage Books in the 1980s and 1990s.

Thanksgiving is rendered to God first of all for His help in preparing this series of books. Without Him we can do nothing. We would also like to thank James W. Beeke for supplying some helpful material; Jenny Luteyn, for contributing several of the stories; Jeff Anderson for his illustrations; and Catherine Mackenzie, for her able and invaluable editing. Finally, we would like to thank our loyal spouses, Mary Beeke and Chris Kleyn, for their love, support, and encouragement as we worked on these books over several years. We pray earnestly that the Lord will bless these stories to many hearts.

Joel R. Beeke and Diana Kleyn
Grand Rapids, Michigan

Contents

How to use this book

The stories within this book and the other titles in the *Building on the Rock* series are all stories with a strong gospel and biblical message. They are ideal for more than one purpose.

1. Devotional Stories: These can be used as a child's own personal devotional time or as part of family worship.

Please note that each story has at least one scripture reference. Every story has a scripture reading referred to at the end which can be used as part of the individual's or the family's Bible reading program. Many of the stories have other references to scripture and some have several extra verses which can also be looked up.

Each story has two prayer points at the end of the book. These are written as helps to prayer and are not to be used as prayers themselves. Reading these pointers should help the child or the family to think about issues connected with the story that need prayer in their own life, the life of their church or the world. Out of the two prayer points written for each story, one prayer point is written specifically for those who have saving faith while the other point is written in such a way that both Christians and non-believers will be brought to pray about their sinful nature and perhaps ask God for His salvation or thank Him for His gift of it.

Each story has also a question and discussion section at the end where the message of the story can either be applied to the reader's life or where a direct question is asked regarding the story itself or a related passage of scripture. The answers to the direct questions are given at the end of the book. Scripture references are indexed at the back of the book. Beside each chapter number you will read the scripture references referred to. These include references within the story, question or scripture reading sections.

2. Children's Talks: As well as all the features mentioned above, the following feature has a particular use for all those involved in giving children's talks at Church, Sunday School, Bible Class, etc. At the end of the series in Book 5, you will find a series index of scripture in biblical order where you will be able to research what books in the series have reference to particular Scriptures. The page number where the Scripture appears is also inserted. Again, all Scriptures from stories, question sections, and Scripture readings are referred to in this section

It is also useful to note that each book will have a section where the reader can determine the length of specific stories beforehand. This will sometimes be useful for devotional times but more often will be a useful feature for those developing a children's talk where they are very dependent on the time available.

Shorter Length Stories

The following stories are shorter in length than the average length of story included in this book. They therefore may be used for family devotions, children's talks, etc. where less time is available:

Longer Length Stories

The following stories are longer in length than the average length of story included in this book. They therefore may be used for family devotions, children's talks, etc. where more time is available:

1. A Hindu Becomes a Christian

Many years ago, an English officer, who was in charge of a British station in India, received a message telling him to return to England for a while. He had quite a few Indian people working for him, and wondered who would be able to take his place while he was gone. He was far away from any missionary station, and there was no other English officer there who he could leave in charge. There was a good deal of valuable property at the station. What should he do? He prayed about it and asked the Lord for guidance.

After thinking and praying about it for a while, the officer decided to ask one of the natives, who lived in the neighborhood, to take charge while he was away. He was a heathen man, since most of the native people were Hindu, but he was respectable, honest, and faithful, and the British officer felt sure that everything would be safe in the care of this man. The man agreed to watch over the station and supervise the workmen as well. Before he left, the officer gave the new supervisor a Bible. He urged him to read it, for in it he would find everything he needed for happiness.

Then the officer went away. He had to go to England, and then to America. More than a year passed before he could return to India. On his homeward journey, the officer wondered how he would find things on his return. He wondered if the man he had left in charge had taken good care of things. He wondered if the workmen had been well cared for, and if everything had gone smoothly. He wondered whether he would hear many complaints and troubles when he returned.

It was a Saturday evening when he got back to his station, and when Sunday morning came, no one knew yet that he had returned. He looked out of his window as soon as he got up in the morning, and was delighted to see how nice everything looked. He felt sure that the man he had left in charge had taken good care of things. Then he began his day with prayer and Bible reading.

At about ten o'clock the officer heard a bell ring. Then he saw some of the workmen as well as some of the villagers gather together at a schoolhouse nearby his house. After a while he heard singing. He wondered what it all meant. He called one of his servants, and asked what they were doing in the schoolhouse. The servant replied that they had church services there now every Sunday.

"Has a missionary been here since I have been away?" asked the officer.

"No, sir," answered the servant.

"Then, who started this church?"

"The 'sahib' (the master) did this while you were away, sir," was the reply.

"And what do they do in church?" inquired the officer, who knew that only one or two others in the village besides himself professed to be Christians.

"They sing, and pray, and then the man reads to them out of the Bible, and talks to the people about salvation in Jesus Christ."

Suddenly, the officer understood! Could this really be the result of the Bible he had given to the new supervisor? This was wonderful news for the British officer. When he left, this man was a heathen. He hated and despised the religion of Jesus. And now, was he really a Christian? The officer hurried over to the schoolhouse. After the service, he spoke to the supervisor, who told him what had happened. He had been curious about what was in the Bible, so he began to read it. The Holy Spirit showed him that he was a sinner, but also that Jesus Christ is the only Savior for sinners. He was led to hate sin, to pray to God, and to love Jesus Christ. He wanted to serve this wonderful Savior. This man became a missionary to his people, preaching the gospel of Jesus Christ wherever he went.

Question: What did the Holy Spirit show the supervisor?
Scripture reading: Acts 8:26-40.

2. A True Minister

Reverend Hans Egede felt that God had called him to preach His Word to the heathen Eskimos who lived in Greenland. This was not possible for some years, but finally, God opened a way. Reverend Egede arrived with a Danish trading company in 1721.

At that time, the Eskimos in Greenland had never heard about the true God or His Word. They were a very fierce people. If a ship was blown to their shore in a storm, they often killed the people and took all the goods on the ship. A human life was not worth much to them.

This was where Reverend Egede landed. He first built a little hut of dirt, stones, and boards for his family in this very cold country. He then tried to learn the Eskimo language. He visited the people in their igloos, which were heated by burning whale oil. The smell was almost unbearable for Reverend Egede, but he continued. He tried to speak to them about God, sin, and salvation in Jesus Christ, but the people only laughed at him.

The trading company decided that they could not work with these people. They told

Reverend Egede to pack his things because they were leaving. He had worked there for two years, but no one had listened to him. But he could not leave so he stayed behind with his family.

More years went by and still there was no change. Then a plague of smallpox broke out. Several Eskimos died from this serious disease. Smallpox is so contagious that no one dared to enter an igloo where someone had the disease. However, Reverend Egede visited and tried to help each sick person. This made a deep impression upon the Eskimos. They saw that it must be an important message which he was bringing. He must be a wonderful man to risk his life in this way. After the plague a few Eskimos came to hear him. Then more and more came. God blessed his preaching and people came to know the Lord Jesus as their Savior. Can you imagine Reverend Egede's joy after working there for so many years? He stayed with the Eskimos for fifteen years and saw a complete change in many people.

Question: This story shows the love and strong desire, found in a true minister's heart, to bring God's Word. Are you interested in God's message that your minister brings to you?
Scripture reading: 1 Corinthians 9:16-23.

3. Follow Jesus' Example

This is a story of a Christian lady who had learned well the lesson of being like Jesus, and of the good she was enabled to do by her example. This lady's name was Miss Bishop. She had been brought up in one of the New England states. Her parents were rich, and she had a very comfortable home with them. She was an earnest Christian woman and she wished to be like Jesus.

Miss Bishop gave herself to missionary work among the Indians in the Northwest. She taught there for some years. The Indians in her school loved and respected her, and well they might, for she had labored most faithfully for their good. She was kind and gentle and patient. Her older scholars had never seen her lose her temper. And when she read and spoke to them about Jesus, they saw that she was following His example. This made them feel sure that the Bible was true.

But some of the scholars, who had not become Christians, felt uncomfortable. Their consciences were troubling them for not wanting to obey God. Miss Bishop's example seemed to be saying to them every day: "The Bible is true. You ought to believe the God of the Bible." And they thought that if they could only see her get angry once, they would not feel so uneasy about it.

So, after school one day, some of the older boys had a meeting to talk about it. They wanted to settle upon a plan to do something that would make Miss Bishop angry. But they could not decide on what to do. They were about to give up when one of the boys, Jimmy Cornplanter, whose little black eyes had been looking intently at the clouds, jumped up and said, "I know, but I'm not going to tell you now. Come tomorrow morning. We will make Miss Bishop mad. She will be very mad!"

None of them believed that Jimmy Cornplanter could make Miss Bishop angry, but they all promised to come.

It was in the middle of the winter, and that winter was an unusually severe one. Early the next morning, Jimmy Cornplanter and the other boys were at the school long before it was time for the teacher to appear. Jimmy told them his plan, which was quickly carried out.

They carried buckets of snow and emptied them into the stove, so that the whole stove was full of snow. Then they hid themselves in the cloak room to wait for the teacher. They were sure she would be very angry to find that she would not be able to start a fire in the stove!

That morning it was bitterly cold. Miss Bishop started out early so she could get a fire going well before school began, to chase the cold out of the schoolhouse. She had to make her own path through the snow, and she was chilled through by the time she reached the schoolhouse. Her fingers ached with cold as she opened the door. She thought for a moment of the comfortable home she had left, where her father, mother, sisters, and brothers had everything they needed for their comfort. But she said to herself, "I am happy to serve Jesus here" and that thought warmed her heart.

She entered the schoolroom, and, taking her little basket of kindling, she opened the door of the stove to start the fire. There, to her amazement, was a pile of snow! She blinked in surprise. Immediately, she suspected it was a trick the boys were playing on her. She did not know they were hidden in the room, watching her. She sighed, but she calmly walked to the door, took the pail and fire-shovel, and patiently set to work to scoop out the snow, without one angry word or impatient look.

This was too much for the boys who had watched it all from their hiding places. They came out looking and feeling rather foolish, but, after asking Miss Bishop's forgiveness, they took the shovel and the pail and soon had all the snow removed. Before long, a fire crackled cheerily in the stove.

This conduct of their teacher had a wonderful effect on the boys, for it was blessed by God. It made them feel sure that what the Bible teaches is true. It made them see that God's work in Miss Bishop's heart was powerful and stronger than man.

During recess that day, Jimmy Cornplanter shouted in triumph to his friends, "Miss Bishop, she can't get mad! Miss Bishop, she can't get mad!" Miss Bishop heard Jimmy and her eyes filled with tears. They could not see her heart — how she prayed for God to make her an example of Christ for these native Indians, and how she worried that she would be a hindrance in the service of her Lord, rather than a useful servant. Now she thanked God and prayed for strength and love to continue this great work of serving God among these Indians.

Question: What was it about Miss Bishop that convinced the boys that what she was saying about God was true?
Scripture reading: Matthew 5:38-48.

4. From Darkness to Light

Mamba was one of the meanest girls in the village and Jymba didn't like her. "I don't care if you are the daughter of my husband's brother," shouted Jymba as she knelt before the small fire in front of her round grass hut in Africa, "you are full of evil spirits!"

"But they are trying to get out of me, and they will, too," retorted Mamba. "See," and she pointed to an ugly, red sore on her right leg.

Mamba used to like being mean—at least, she thought she enjoyed it. But one day two white "spirits" came to their village. She knew now that they were really a white man and his wife from far across the sea. The first time they had come, Mamba and the other village children, thinking they were from the spirit world, hid in terror.

The missionaries had spoken beautiful, unforgettable words. Mamba and the others had finally crept out of their hiding places to listen. The man said the story they told was from a Book which came from heaven and was true. It was a story of a new God, new to Mamba, but known to other men and women in other parts of the world for ages and ages.

This God was truly an ancient One, for the white man said He had always lived.

The missionaries told, too, of this Great One's love for those who worshipped Him. They said this God loved His people so much that He had given His only Son to die for them. They said that Mamba must repent and ask this God to forgive her many sins, for the sake of His Son whose name was Jesus. Those who repented of their sins and believed in His Name would live forever with Him in a beautiful place called heaven. The blood of His Son, Jesus Christ, could wash away all sins. No one was too bad. When Mamba heard that, she thought, "They don't know how bad I am! I wonder if even I could be made good by this powerful One?" A longing to belong to this great God filled her heart. But just then she spied a little red purse that belonged to the missionary lady and she stole it.

Since then, when the missionaries called at her village, Mamba listened to their message from a safe hiding place. She did not dare to be seen. The more she heard, the more she saw how sinful she was. If the missionaries saw her, they would see her guilt for sure. She could not hide from God. The missionaries said that He could see her all the time, even when she did wrong things. This God could even see inside her—He knew her very thoughts.

Mamba had forgotten Jymba for a moment as she thought about the missionaries and the stories they had told. But now she jumped as her angry aunt spoke again. "Sawana told me you were lazy and didn't work at all today. He said you lay in the tall grass beside the peanut field and just looked at the sky."

"I was not being lazy. My leg was hurting me!" said Mamba.

"And he said you scratched and bit Matemo's little sister and stole her string of tiger's teeth. What can I do with such a lazy, mean child? Just get out of my sight! There is no place for you here tonight!" Her eyes blazed with anger.

This wasn't the first night Mamba had been forced to stay out all night. It wasn't the first time she had gone without supper. Sawana was always fed first, and he was very greedy. Many nights, she had only a few scraps for her supper.

Mamba tossed her head in the air and walked away from Jymba's grass hut as though she were the daughter of the chief, instead of the little orphan girl she was, whom no one wanted or cared for.

She would go to Ndombo's hut. Ndombo and his wife had listened to the missionaries too. Their place was clean and they would share their evening meal with her. There wasn't room in their hut for her, but they would give her a mat and let her sleep just outside their door. She would get to see their baby too. And maybe Ndombo's wife would teach her the song she sang to the baby. She had learned the song from the missionary lady. Ndombo told Mamba that the songs of their people were all sad, for their hearts had no hope. But the missionaries' songs told of hope in Jesus for this life and the life to come.

As darkness came over the land, Mamba lay on the hard ground outside Ndombo's hut, but she could not go to sleep. Her leg hurt too much. She lay there thinking of when she first came to this village three years ago. Her uncle hadn't wanted her, but he felt he had to take her in because she was his brother's child, and his brother was dead now. Jymba, his wife, had always hated her; she thought of her as just another mouth to feed. Sawana, their son, was cruel to her.

Mamba felt so alone. There was no one in all the world who loved her. No one cared whether she lived or died. There was no one to feed or care for her. She was kicked and beaten and yelled at from morning till night.

Mamba had been taught that everybody was full of evil spirits. These evil spirits were trying to harm every person and every animal. They were even living in stones and in trees and bushes. One had to be very brave to sleep out in the open where these evil spirits could harm you. So Mamba didn't enjoy the beautiful moonlight and starlight above her, nor the beauty of the palm trees against the sky. She believed that evil spirits were lurking about ready to pounce on her!

"The evil ones are trying hard to get out of me tonight," thought Mamba as her leg ached and throbbed with pain. Just a week ago, the witch doctor had sent for Jymba. Jymba found the witch doctor sitting in his dark, dirty hut with all his fetishes, charms and medicines around him. "Mamba has evil spirits living in her," he said. "I will call them out, but you must give me one of your chickens."

Jymba hesitated a minute. Mamba was not worth a chicken, but the witch doctor looked so mean that Jymba feared he would cast a magic spell over her if she did not give him the chicken, so she said he could have it.

That night the witch doctor crept to Jymba's hut after Mamba was asleep. He muttered strange words with weird sounds and waved his arms in strange motions. Jymba and Sawana looked on with eyes full of fear. Then he cut the skin of Mamba's right leg to let the evil spirits out. Mamba awoke with a cry of pain and fear. But Jymba told her the evil spirits could get out of her now. Mamba believed that the open sore would allow the evil spirits to leave her body. Although that had happened a week ago, every day since then her leg hurt more and more. Now it was a big open wound.

Mamba lay staring into the black shadows of the night. The missionaries had told her people to pray to the great God in heaven. He alone could save them from all harm and evil. He could even give her a new heart. Then she would love and serve Him. But her heart was so bad. Did she dare to pray to the God who was so holy and good? The darkness of the night seemed to close in, and Mamba felt hopelessly lost. Closing her eyes tightly, she stammered her first prayer. "Oh, God of the missionaries," she prayed, "save me from the dark, and take the darkness from my heart. Please, save me."

Late in the night, Mamba fell into a restless sleep. The next morning, she lay on the ground outside Ndombo's hut burning with fever. She was moaning and saying strange things and didn't know where she was. The infection from her leg had gone through her whole body. Mamba was a very sick girl.

On the way to his peanut field, Ndombo stopped at Jymba's hut and told her about Mamba. Jymba said she would send Sawana to carry her home.

Jymba went to the mat where Sawana was sleeping and shook him. "Wake up, my son. There is something you must do quickly." Sawana sat up on his mat, and his mother whispered to him, "You remember how the witch doctor had Mbangu kill their only goat and sprinkle the blood toward heaven when their son was dying. Mamba is sick, perhaps dying, and she is not worth a goat. That worthless one has already cost me a chicken. Go to Ndombo's house and pick her up. Make believe you are carrying her here, but take her to the edge of the jungle. We will say she did not know what she was doing and wandered off there by herself."

And Sawana, cruel boy that he was, went to do as his mother bade him.

Mamba was so sick that she did not know when Sawana picked her up. She did not know when they left the village nor when she was laid at the edge of the jungle where poisonous snakes crawled and where wild animals stalked, looking for prey. Mamba did not hear the soft pad of tiger feet, nor did she see the gleaming yellow eyes look at her. She did not know when the tiger crouched for his spring upon her. But God in heaven saw, and not one minute too soon, not one minute too late, He had His servant walk that way.

It was the day for the missionary and his wife to visit Mamba's village. To reach it they had to walk close to the jungle for some distance. The keen eye of the white man saw the big cat stalking some object on the ground. He saw him crouch for the kill, but the white man was fast. He was carrying his gun in the crook of his arm and quick as a flash he raised it, pulled the trigger and the tiger rolled over dead.

The missionary took Mamba to the mission compound in a village several miles away. There she was washed till her skin shone. Then she was put to bed on a clean mat, and for the first time in her life she could wear a clean white nightgown.

Much prayer was offered for the sick girl. The constant care and love were blessed and soon she began to recover. Her body was so starved that she thought she could never get enough of the good soup. And her heart was so starved that she thought she could never get enough love. They gave her plenty of both at the mission station. They especially told her how God in His providence had spared her life from the crouching tiger, and healed her from her terrible sickness and infection. The Lord blessed these instructions to her young heart. She learned to read the Bible and the Holy Spirit taught its truths to her soul. Mamba experienced the great wonder of God's grace in reaching out to save such an evil one as she was.

Mamba often went to her own village to tell her people about the missionaries' God and His Son Jesus. Jymba and Sawana looked at her in amazement. She looked so healthy and clean. When she read her book to them, Sawana said, "Mamba knows white magic. She makes the little marks talk words." Now they have heard the message of the Bible, too. And Mamba is praying for them every day, that they too will be freed from superstition and feel their need for the Lord Jesus Christ.

Question: What did Mamba get plenty of at the mission station? What did she learn there? What did Mamba pray for?
Scripture reading: Acts 14:1-18.

5. Kimbu

A missionary and his wife, with their small son, were sent to Africa. They set up a tiny mission post in the jungle. They learned the language of the natives, and tried to tell them of their need for the Lord Jesus. The people listened, and even though a few seemed to believe his words, they did not stop their heathen idol worship.

After two years, the missionary started a small school. He invited the natives to bring their children. The children loved their missionary-teacher. He taught them so many wonderful things, and told them so many nice stories! One boy seemed especially interested in the Bible stories. Sometimes the missionary saw tears in Kimbu's eyes.

One day after school the missionary sat at his desk, preparing his lessons for the next day. When he glanced up from his work, he noticed Kimbu standing in the doorway.

"Come in, Kimbu," said the missionary kindly. "Is something wrong? Is anyone sick in your family?" The missionary was also a doctor.

Kimbu looked seriously into the missionary's face. "My heart is bad, Teacher."

"Why do you say that, Kimbu?"

"I have so many sins, I do bad things; I think bad things."

"Does that make you sad?" asked the teacher.

"Yes. I make God sad, too." Tears formed in Kimbu's brown eyes, and rolled down his dark cheeks.

"Listen, Kimbu. You have heard me tell you about the One who can save sinners. He is the Lord Jesus."

"But Jesus is your God!" cried Kimbu. "He won't listen to me. I'm not a white boy."

"Kimbu!" exclaimed the missionary. "The Lord Jesus came to save lost sinners, no matter what color their skin is."

"How do you know?" demanded Kimbu.

"Did you ever ask Him to give you a clean heart?" asked the missionary.

"Yes, and I just feel worse."

"Kimbu, the Lord wants to show you your wicked heart before He makes you feel you have a clean heart. He wants you to know why you need a new heart."

"When will He help me?" asked Kimbu tearfully.

"I don't know that, Kimbu," answered the missionary. "But don't stop asking Him to help you. He wants you to ask Him for a new heart. When you are all alone, you may tell the Lord just what you are feeling. The Lord will listen."

The missionary prayed with the little boy, and then Kimbu left. The missionary added his own prayer, asking the Lord for wisdom, and for Kimbu's conversion.

For the next few days Kimbu was very quiet and thoughtful at school. Often, instead of playing with other children, he would ask to read in the "Children's Bible" that the missionary let the children read.

The missionary and his wife chose Bible stories they thought might help Kimbu, but the boy remained quiet and withdrawn.

One afternoon as the missionary was teaching the children a lesson on African elephants, there was a knock on the door, and a native rushed into the room.

"Your baby is very sick. Your wife say come."

For a second, the missionary looked frightened. He could hardly believe it. That morning before he had left for school he had played with his son who was perfectly healthy. He realised that there were fourteen children waiting for his reaction. He wished he could run home, but he couldn't leave these children sitting here. He prayed silently for help.

The missionary turned to the native still standing in the doorway. "Tell Ellen I am coming. First I will pray with the children."

Very simply the teacher laid his need before the Lord, asking him to heal his son. Then he prayed for the children, asking the Lord to protect them. Calmly the missionary dismissed them, and then he hurried home. "What's wrong with the baby?"

"He stopped breathing. I followed all the steps you taught me, and he started breathing soon after that, but it really scared me," his wife said.

The missionary had already grabbed his doctor's bag from the bedroom as his wife talked and was examining the little boy. "He'll be OK," he said with relief.

It was then that they noticed Kimbu standing in the doorway. "How is your boy?" he asked with concern.

"He's fine now, Kimbu," smiled the missionary. "He stopped breathing, but the Lord helped him to breathe again. He is very tired now, but God will make him well again."

Kimbu looked at the teacher in amazement. To him that meant God had awakened the baby from death. He tiptoed to the crib and stared at the sleeping baby. "God heard me and you," he whispered. "I asked God to make the baby better. God listened to me."

Kimbu ran from the house before the missionary or his wife could respond. They thanked the Lord for sparing their child, and they also prayed again for Kimbu's conversion.

The next morning before the missionary set out for school, Kimbu entered the house. "I pray to the Lord now, Teacher. I ask your God to be my God, too."

The missionary and his wife were very glad to hear this, and they prayed that God would truly change his heart.

A few months later the missionary sat at his desk in the schoolroom while the children played outside before the school day began. His thoughts were interrupted by the loud voice of Takiki, the biggest student in the mission school. Takiki was saying, "Kimbu, you serve a strange God. Show me the God that you serve."

The missionary heard Kimbu's little voice bravely answer, "I cannot show you the God I serve, but I can show you the god you serve."

The missionary quietly got up from his chair and watched Kimbu take a block of wood that was lying on the ground. Then he took a handful of mud from a puddle and slapped it on the block in several places to make a face. "There, Takiki, that is the dead god you serve."

A few days after this, Takiki brought the subject up again. The clearing around the schoolhouse was so small that the missionary could hear exactly what went on when he was sitting at his desk.

The teacher had given each child five marbles. They had never seen marbles before, and they were greatly valued by the children. Some children had stolen from each other, and Kimbu had told them that that was wrong.

Takiki began to tease Kimbu, "We can't

even see your God, so how can He see us?" Pointing to an idol at the edge of the clearing, he said, "Our god sees us, but he doesn't care if we steal."

All the children watched as Kimbu took some mud and walked over to the idol. Then he rubbed the mud over the eyes of the image and said, "Your god can't see, and he must be a dead god if he lets me rub mud in his eyes."

Kimbu was often teased, but God gave him the strength to stand these tests of faith. Later the children began to respect him, although not all of them stopped their idol worship.

Question: How many gods are there? Read about this in 1 Corinthians 8:4-6. What does Habakkuk 2:18-20 teach you about idols? Scripture Reading: 1 Kings 18:20-40.

6. Not Home Yet

It was late afternoon as the large ocean liner sailed into port at New York City with its many passengers. Most of them were on deck and standing by the rail as preparations were being made to dock. Many were returning from business or pleasure trips abroad; others were arriving in the United States for the first time. Some had been away from home for many years, like the missionary and his wife who had spent many years of their life in a remote region in far-away Africa.

As they stood by the ship's rail, they looked longingly at the shore of their beloved country. They wondered who would be there to meet them. They had been away so long. They had worked hard for many years where no one saw them but their God. It had not been easy, but for not one moment would they have been anywhere else, for it was where the Lord had sent them. But now, with their health broken and the years of toil showing in their faces, they were coming home.

The missionary had written to his church in New York, telling them that they would be coming. When they left Africa, they had not received a letter from New York, but mail was slow, and they didn't worry.

They peered eagerly toward the docks now, and were astounded to see thousands of people, waiting for the ship, crying, "Welcome home!" They seemed to be pointing to where the missionaries were standing.

"Do all those people know we are coming home?" the missionary asked.

"I'm sure I don't know," his wife replied.

The crowd continued to shout as the ship eased into its berth, and amid the noise and music of the band the missionaries could now hear more clearly what they were

saying. They were welcoming home a great game hunter from one of his hunting trips to Africa! The missionaries looked at each other, and then started down the gangplank to the dock where the crowd was pushing and shoving to get a glimpse of the great game hunter. But there was no one to meet the missionaries!

Later, as they were riding silently in a taxi on their way to the hotel, Satan the accuser whispered to the old missionary, "See how they greet the men of the world, and you, one of God's preachers whose life has been given to preaching the gospel in the dangerous jungle, do not have a single person to welcome you home!"

This man of God admitted in his heart that he was terribly disappointed, and Satan continued to taunt him as he sat sadly in his hotel room. "No one to greet you! No one cares!" continued to ring in his head.

Finally, he said to his wife, "After all these years, my dear, I thought there would be someone to greet us, someone to welcome us home!"

His wife answered sweetly, "I know, dear. I'm going out for a while. Talk to God about it and see what He says."

Left alone in that lonely hotel room, the old missionary bowed his head and did just that. All the things Satan had said, and implied, were poured out in childlike simplicity to his Father in heaven.

Some time later his wife returned, and

as she entered the room, she noticed the serene expression on her husband's face.

"Well, dear, what did He say?" she asked.

In response, the old missionary quoted John 14:1-3: "'Let not your heart be troubled: ye believe in God, believe also in me. In my Father's house are many mansions: if it were not so, I would have told you. I go to prepare a place for you. And if I go and prepare a place for you, I will come again and receive you unto myself; that where I am, there ye may be also.' He said to me," wept the missionary, "My child, you're not home yet!"

Question: Where is a Christian's real home?
What encouragement is there in Colossians 3:23-24 for missionaries and those who have given their lives to God's service?
Scripture reading: Revelation 21:1-6.

7. The Eyes of the Chief

Evening was coming, and the sun was disappearing swiftly behind the dark treetops of the Xhosa mountains in South Africa. A last golden glow shone over the white walls of the mission post "Moria."

As the last sunlight still glowed through the windows of the children's ward of the mission hospital, Dr. Everts, the missionary, looked down the length of the ward. He saw many black Zulu children with their dark, curly heads and shining black eyes.

The sick children sat or lay on their beds, with their black hands folded on the white sheets, waiting for the evening prayer. The missionary prayed with them, asking the Lord to heal them from their sicknesses and to send the light of the gospel in their dark hearts.

When he was ready to leave the ward, a little black hand stretched out to him, and a longing child's voice said, "Doctor, Doctor!"

He stopped and answered, "Yes?"

"Doctor," said the child, "when will it be Christmas? Will you come to tell us a Bible story then?"

The missionary smiled, "Yes, I promise to tell you about the shepherds and their flocks of sheep, and about the great Light in the dark night. If the sun shines two more times, then it will be Christmas. But now you must go to sleep."

From the hospital, Dr. Everts walked to his own house. There was happiness in his heart. He would be able to tell the wonderful story of Jesus Christ's birth from the Bible to so many heathen children.

He looked at the disappearing sun which glowed over the mountain tops. Far away on top of the highest mountain, he saw the Zulu village, Kakoela. Chief Chuana, the upper-chief of the whole mountain territory, lived there. When he looked at that village, he was filled with sorrow.

Chief Chuana had much power. All the inhabitants of the mountains obeyed him. No one dared to come to the mission hospital for the Chief had forbidden it. Mothers who brought their children to the "Moria" mission post would be punished by him and would not receive any food for many days.

The missionary had often asked Chief Chuana whether he could come and tell the people in his village about the Bible and help the sick. But the Chief was angry and full of enmity. He had forbidden that.

Now the days of Christmas were coming. In many lands and churches the glad message of the gospel was being brought.

He had a longing to bring the glad tidings also to the people of Kakoela.

He knew that the women and children in the Kakoela mountain village had a great fear of evil spirits. The children lived in constant fear that they would be killed by the spirits. If they were sick and had a stomachache or headache they thought that there was an evil spirit or a serpent in their stomach or head. Then they would hit themselves very hard to chase that evil spirit out. Of course that did not help. Instead, they felt still more pain and became more afraid.

Children from Kakoela and from the mountains did not know that long ago the angels sang in Bethlehem's fields, "Fear not: for, behold, I bring you good tidings of great joy, which shall be to all people. For unto you is born this day in the city of David a Saviour, which is Christ the Lord."(Luke 2:10-11)

The missionary desired to go to the mountain village of the Chief. He wanted to tell the people there that the witch doctors were liars, and that only the great King, the Lord Jesus Christ, could take away their fear, agony, and sins. Would he ever be allowed to enter the village of Kakoela?

That evening, the missionary and his wife knelt for prayer in their little house. The missionary begged the Lord to show His power and open the way for him to go to Kakoela. "Perhaps I may go tomorrow already," he said to his wife hopefully.

The following morning he sent a messenger to the Chief to ask whether the doctor could come and visit the people in Kakoela. But the messenger came back very frightened.

The Chief was furious! He did not want any Christians in his village. The Book of the white man was not allowed to come to Kakoela. Dr. Everts did his work that day feeling disappointed, and yet there was hope in his heart that he could yet go to Kakoela.

It was the afternoon of Christmas Day. After checking the patients in the hospital, Dr. Everts walked to his own home. A panting Zulu boy suddenly stood before him. Gasping for breath, he said, "Oh doctor, you must come at once to Kakoela! The eyes of the Chief are dead. Now he cannot do any more work."

Alarmed, Dr. Everts asked, "Are the eyes of the Chief Chuana very sick?"

"No, no," said the boy, "they are dead, and you must come quickly to give light in the dead eyes again, for the Chief cannot make his journey now."

The doctor got his instrument bag ready and told the head nurse, "Please get a room in the hospital ready for the Chief." Then he put a stretcher in the back of his car. He was soon on the narrow, bumpy mountain road with two of the helpers from the hospital. He was on his way to the village of the Chief.

Many things were in the thoughts of the missionary. Suddenly he was allowed to go to Kakoela on Christmas Day. But he had wanted to go for a very different reason. He had hoped that he would be allowed to tell those people the message of Jesus' birth. But now he had to come for the eyes of the Chief, in which there was no light anymore. This was very serious. During the ride he thought about how he would speak to the Chief. With great anxiety, he entered the little village of Kakoela.

Chief Chuana stood at the entrance of the village, dressed in his fine red cloak, waiting for him. As the missionary looked anxiously at him, he immediately saw two bright, commanding eyes staring at him. Dr. Everts did not understand. After the long African greeting, he asked the Chief, "Are your eyes sick?"

"Yes," said the Chief, "I will show them to you." The doctor felt very puzzled by the Chief's answer, but he followed him outside the "kraal." There stood an old freight truck. The Chief pointed to the headlights and said, "Look, the eyes are dead. They will not look anymore. Now I cannot use him. Can you put new light in them?"

Very surprised, the missionary said, "Oh, the eyes of your truck are dead! Your messenger came to tell me that the eyes of the Chief are dead! I have come quickly only to find that the lights of your car give no light. Why did you let your boy tell me that your eyes were without light?"

Then it was the Chief's turn to be puzzled. He said, "That car is mine, so the eyes are mine, too." Dr. Everts tried to explain to Chief Chuana that a doctor can only be called for sick eyes of people from the village, not for the dead eyes of his car.

Dr. Everts was very disappointed. He had made a long, difficult journey over a bumpy mountain road and thought, "Did I have to come all the way up here for this, on Christmas Day?"

Chief Chuana urgently asked the doctor to repair the eyes of his car. In hopes of gaining the friendship of the Chief, the missionary checked the car lights. He soon found the problem. After making a small repair, the lights were in good working order again. The Chief was very glad that the eyes could see again.

He ordered the women to prepare some food for the doctor. Wood was brought and soon a fire was kindled in front of Chuana's hut. All the men and boys gathered around the fire. The women and girls sat at a distance in a wide circle behind the men. After the doctor ate the food, Chief Chuana commanded all the people of the village to gather around the fire. To show his thankfulness for healing the eyes of his truck, he, the mighty Chief, gave the missionary permission to tell something out of the Book of his King just this once.

Dr. Everts felt ashamed. His disappointment fled as he understood that the Lord, by the strange message of blind eyes, had brought him to Kakoela on Christmas Day. It became an unforgettable evening.

In the dark, warm quietness of the African evening, Chief Chuana, all his wives, the men, women, and children of Kakoela sat around the fire. All those dark eyes were fixed on the white man as they gave him their full attention. The missionary saw their dark faces shining in the light of the flames, and a deep love and pity for their souls filled his heart. For a moment he sat with bowed head and folded hands among those Kakoela people. The missionary prayed for help and wisdom from the Lord.

Then he raised his head, looked at the people, and told them the wonderful story of Jesus' birth from the Holy Book. He told them the history of the King of kings, who came as the Light in the darkness of a sinful world.

He told them, "Your souls are as dead eyes. That is why you cannot believe the Word of God. But if the almighty God touches your souls and quickens them, then light will come in place of your darkness. Then your souls will be as eyes with light. Then you will be able to understand God's Word and you will desire that you may see by faith that great Light, Jesus Christ. You will desire to be saved by Him from eternal darkness."

It was already late in the evening when the missionary finished his story. It was perfectly quiet. Chief Chuana arose. He thanked Dr. Everts for the wonderful words spoken and asked him to come back and give them more of the good words of the Book. It had become an unforgettable Christmas Day for the people of Kakoela and also for the missionary.

It was almost dark when he returned to the mission post. The head nurse was glad when she heard that the Chief was healthy. But she was especially happy that the children of Kakoela had heard the gospel message for the first time in their lives.

Tell all the world His wondrous ways,
Tell heathen nations far and near;
Great is the Lord, and great His praise,
And Him alone let nations fear.

Question: What is wrong with your soul if it doesn't trust in the Lord Jesus Christ?
Scripture reading: Luke 2:10-11,
1 Corinthians 2:6-16.

8. The Indian's Revenge

The beautiful rule, "Whatsoever ye would that men should do to you, do ye even so to them," (Matthew 7:12) is taken from Christ's sermon on the mount, and should be obeyed by all. Unless we are His children, we can never observe this great command as we ought.

Many years ago, on the outskirts of one of the pioneer settlements, was a small but neat cottage which belonged to an industrious farmer. He was only a boy when he had left England to travel with his family to America. He had helped his father build his homestead, plant his crops, and care for the cattle. Now that he was married, he worked on his own farm.

It was a lovely, quiet place. The cabin was built on a small hill which sloped toward a stream which turned a large sawmill situated a little further downstream. The garden produced various kinds of vegetables, which would soon be preserved for the long cold winter. On the hillside was an orchard with several kinds of fruit trees. The fields of hay stood ready to be harvested, and the corn was just coming into the ear. Further on were the forests which provided fine hunting grounds. The farmer and his wife had been richly blessed.

It was a lovely summer evening. The sun had set, though the sky still glowed with the brilliant colors of the sunset. William Sullivan, the farmer, sat on the doorstep of his cabin, sharpening his scythes for the coming hay season. He was a kind-hearted man, but he was filled with prejudice against the North American Indians. Ever since he was a boy he had heard false and exaggerated stories of the "wild savages," the Indians who lived in the plains and forests of America. He despised them as ruthless heathens, forgetting that he himself never thanked God for the blessing he had so richly received.

William was so intent on sharpening his scythes that he did not hear the approach of the tall Indian until he heard his question: "Will you please give me some supper and a place to sleep tonight? I have had no success in hunting today."

The young farmer raised his head and a look of contempt covered his face. With an angry scowl he said bitterly, "You heathen Indian dog, I will give you nothing! Go away!"

The Indian turned away, but then stopped: "Sir, I am very hungry, for it is a long time since I have eaten. Give me only a crust of bread to strengthen me for the rest of my journey."

William stood up. "Get away from me, you heathen dog! I have nothing for you!"

A struggle seemed to take place within the Indian, as though pride and need were battling each other. His need for food and drink won, and he pleaded, "Just a cup of cold water, please? I feel faint."

"There's plenty of water in the river. Now get out of here!" shouted William.

With a proud but sad air, the Indian turned away and slowly walked toward the little river. His weak steps showed plainly that his need was great.

What neither William nor the Indian knew, was that Mary, the farmer's wife, had heard the Indian's request and her husband's rude replies as she rocked her infant to sleep. Through the little window she saw the Indian's faltering steps, and saw him fall to the ground in exhaustion. Glancing toward the barn, she saw that her husband was on his way there to check the animals. Quickly she gathered some milk, leftover supper, and some bread. Then she hurried to the Indian who lay with his eyes closed.

"Will my brother drink some milk?" she asked softly.

He gladly received the food and milk Mary brought him. When he had finished, the Indian spoke his gratitude. "Carcoochee will protect the white dove from the pounces of the eagle. For her sake, the young will be safe in its nest, and her red brother will not seek revenge."

Pulling a bunch of heron's feathers from his buckskin tunic, he selected the longest one and gave it to Mary Sullivan. "When the white dove's man flies over the Indian's hunting grounds, tell him to wear this on his head." Then he turned away, and disappeared into the forest.

The summer passed, harvest had come and gone, and Mary had preserved an abundance of vegetables and fruit from the garden and the orchard. The pumpkins were safely stored away, and the trees glowed with the rich colors of autumn. William Sullivan and others in the pioneer settlement began making plans for a hunting trip. It was always a time of great excitement, and William usually had no fear of the Indian attacks which they heard about occasionally. He was an expert hunter, well able to handle his rifle and his hatchet.

But this time, doubts filled his mind. In his dreams, he often saw the face of the Indian whom he had treated so shamefully several months earlier. The evening before he was to leave on the hunting trip, he confessed his fears to his wife.

"Mary," he said, "I keep thinking about that Indian. My conscience won't stop bothering me. Everything my mother ever taught me about my duty to my neighbor keeps running through my mind. It makes me feel awful. I feel as though God is angry with me because I did not help a suffering man created by God."

Mary listened in silence to her husband. When he was finished, she laid her hand in his and looked into his face with a nervous smile. "I have something to tell you. I didn't dare say anything earlier because of the angry way you spoke to the Indian."

She told him how she had helped the exhausted Indian. Then she walked over to the desk in the corner and took out the beautiful heron's feather. She told him the words that Carcoochee, the Indian, had spoken to her as he handed her the feather.

"You don't need to fear revenge if you wear this feather, William," she said.

"Indians never forget a wrong done to them," answered her husband sadly.

"Neither do they ever forget a kindness," she reminded him. "I will sew this feather in your hunting cap, and then trust you to God's keeping. My father used to say that we must never forget the lawful means for our safety."

Mary sewed quietly for a few minutes, and then shyly spoke. "William," she began, "now that my dear father is gone, I think often of all the things he tried to teach me. I'm afraid I haven't taken his teachings to heart."

"What do you mean, Mary? You are a wonderful wife and mother," said William.

"But we are not living as we should. If God were to treat us as we have been treating Him, He would have to leave us to ourselves because we have forgotten Him."

Tears filled Mary's eyes as she spoke. She was the only daughter of a godly English sailor. When she was a child, she seemed tender toward the things of the Lord. But when she met William Sullivan, her profession of religion vanished since he was not a godly man, although he was kind, decent, and hard working.

Over the years, Mary's conscience had spoken, and since the incident with Carcoochee, her heart was troubled and could find no rest. The Holy Spirit of God was at work in her heart, and He was showing her that without God there is no peace. Day after day He brought to her memory the truths she had learned in her childhood.

Now, for the first time, Mary and William acknowledged that they needed to seek the Lord. They talked together somewhat shyly about these things, happy to discover they shared the same concerns. That evening the young couple knelt together in prayer for the first time in their married life.

The morning the hunters left was a beautiful one. There was not a cloud in the sky as William said goodbye to his wife. William's fears were gone, and Mary and their little son waved cheerfully as William set off with the others. He had wanted to remove the heron feather from his cap, but gave in when Mary begged him to keep it.

The hunters were successful. Several animals were killed, and at night the hunters took shelter in the cave of a bear that one of the hunters had shot. After a delicious supper of roasted meat, the hunters settled down to sleep.

With the first light of dawn, the hunters were up, ready for another day of hunting. Soon William glimpsed a deer, and followed silently. So intent was he on following the deer that he did not realize how far he had traveled away from the others. To William's disappointment, the deer got away, but when he tried to find his way back, nothing seemed familiar. The trees of the forest were so thick, and the underbrush so dense that he could barely even catch a glimpse of the sun. Further and further he wandered, trying to find a familiar place. As the hours went by, he became frightened and imagined he heard and saw hostile Indians. William prayed that God would help him find his way back to the others, but he worried that God would not answer him. He did not deserve God's help.

Toward sunset, the trees thinned out, and he found himself on the outskirts of a vast prairie covered with tall grasses. Here and there were patches of small trees and brush. A river ran through the prairie, and William made his way toward it. He was tired and thirsty, not having eaten anything since breakfast early that morning.

At the bank of the river there were many bushes, and William approached cautiously, holding his gun ready for danger. When he was only a few feet from the riverbank, he heard some rustling, and suddenly an enormous buffalo charged out from the bushes. These animals usually roamed on the prairies in herds, but sometimes one

became separated from the herd. The buffalo paused for a moment, and then, lowering his enormous head, rushed forward at the intruder.

William took aim with his rifle, but the animal was too close for him to aim carefully. The shot merely grazed the buffalo, which only made it furious. Desperately, William drew his hunting knife, hoping to cut the animal's throat. But the buffalo shook him off easily and threw William to the ground. The huge animal turned, ready to charge again when the sharp crack of a rifle sounded behind William. The buffalo sprang into the air, then fell heavily, close to where William lay.

In the gathering darkness, the form of an Indian appeared. William wondered whether or not the Indian would be friendly.

"If the weary hunter will rest until morning, the eagle will show him the way to the nest of his white dove," the Indian said.

Without another word, the Indian led him to a small encampment near the river. Here the Indian gave William some Indian corn and venison. Then he showed him some animal skins where he could sleep.

The light of dawn had not yet appeared on the horizon when the Indian awoke William. After a quick breakfast, they started out. The Indian walked in front with a confidence which told William how well he knew the forest. They walked until late afternoon, and then William stood within view of his beloved home. With happy tears in his eyes, William started to thank the Indian.

The Indian, who until then had not allowed his face to be seen by William except in the dim light of his wigwam, now faced him. William was astonished to see that it was the same Indian whom he had treated so cruelly several months earlier. An expression of dignified, yet mild rebuke was evident in Carcoochee's face as he looked at the bewildered farmer, but his voice was gentle as he spoke.

"Five moons ago, when I was faint and weary, you called me 'Indian dog' and told me to go away. I might have had my revenge last night, but the white dove fed me, and for her sake I spared you. Carcoochee bids you go home, and when you see other Indians in need of kindness, do to them as I have done to you."

He lifted his hand and turned to leave, but William begged him not to leave. "Mary would love to thank you too," he said.

At last, Carcoochee consented, and the humbled farmer led him to his cabin. There Mary thanked the Indian with tears in her eyes. Carcoochee was treated as an honored guest and a brother. Carcoochee paid many visits to the little cabin at the edge of the forest. William, once prejudiced against the Indians, now loved Carcoochee as a brother. The "heathen Indian" taught William a lesson of kindness which William should have known already. The Lord used this experience with Carcoochee to show him his own wicked heart. William saw that he was a sinner in the sight of God. William was led by the Holy Spirit to feel his need of Christ's atoning blood, and before many months passed, both he and Mary Sullivan showed by their words and actions that they were born again.

Carcoochee's kindness was repaid to him a hundredfold. A long time passed before any change of heart was visible in him, but it pleased the Lord to bless the patient teaching of William and Mary Sullivan to their friend's soul. The Lord answered the Sullivans' prayers, and converted Carcoochee.

Carcoochee was the first Indian to be baptized by an American missionary who came about two years later to a mission post several miles from the Sullivans' home. After several years of Bible study, Carcoochee became a missionary to the Indians, telling them the gospel of Jesus Christ. For many years he worked among his people before he died and went to be with his Lord and Savior, leaving behind a clear testimony of the love he had for his Redeemer.

Question: What did Carcoochee and William have in common before they came to know the Lord? What did they have in common after they came to know the Lord?
Scripture reading: 2 Samuel 9.

9. How God Stopped the Pirates

S

The English ship, the *Britannia*, was sailing from London to the West Indies. There were missionaries on board, hoping to teach the natives there about Jesus Christ. One day they saw a pirate vessel bearing down on them. The captain of the English ship quickly shouted orders to the crew to defend the *Britannia* as best they could. But while they got ready to fight, the missionaries went to their cabins to pray. They knew they could do more good in that way than in any other.

The pirate ship drew nearer. As soon as it was within range, the pirates began to fire. They had their grappling irons ready. These were strong, sharp hooks, attached to long ropes, which, when thrown into the other ship, would hold her fast while the pirates came on board to rob and murder.

The captain of the English vessel saw no chance of escape. His heart sank at the thought of what would happen to them. He did not know what powerful helpers he had in those few praying missionaries. But amid all the noise of the battle, the prayers of these missionaries were going up to heaven.

The pirates tried to throw their grappling irons across to the English ship, but just at that moment, their own ship gave a violent lurch, and the men who held the irons were thrown into the sea. The pirates tried again, but the same thing happened again. Then they tried to fire at the *Britannia* until she sank. But they failed in this also. Sometimes the cannonballs would miss and fall into the sea. At other times, the dense smoke from the discharge of the guns would hang strangely about the pirate ship, so that the pirates could not see where the other vessel was. At last, after another round of gunfire, a sudden gust of wind cleared away the curtain of smoke which had been hanging around the pirate ship, and the pirate captain saw, to his amazement, the *Britannia* with her sails spread in the wind, carried away from him and out of his reach.

Five years later, the captain met those missionaries on the island of St. Thomas. He was a pirate no longer, but a Christian. He told them that the wonderful way in which the English ship had escaped him was the first thing that led him to think seriously about his wicked life. God's ways are perfect. "The righteous cry, and the LORD heareth, and delivereth them out of all their troubles" (Psalm 34:17).

Question: What did the missionaries do and why did it make a difference?
Scripture reading: Psalm 34.

10. The Missionary and the Hyena

Bishop Gobat, before he was made a bishop of Jerusalem, was a missionary among the Druses in the mountains of Lebanon, and other tribes in the wildest parts of Syria. One day a messenger came to him from a heathen chief, begging him to come to him and tell him about the religion of Jesus Christ. This was good news to the missionary. He sent word to the chief that he would come and visit him in a few days.

But the next day, Mr Gobat became sick, and could not visit the chief. The chief sent another messenger with a more earnest invitation. The missionary told him he would go to visit him the next day, and he prepared for the journey. Just as he was leaving his little house, however, a letter arrived for him saying that the ship he had bought a ticket for was sailing the next day at noon. What was he going to do? Would he have enough time to bring the gospel to the heathen chief?

The messenger told him that if they set out at once, he would be able to spend the night with the chief, and still reach the ship in time if he left early the next day. So

Mr. Gobat started out with the messenger and some of the natives. The journey took them through the woods, and over the mountains. At one of the villages on the way, they were delayed several hours, to visit someone in need. Then they lost their way, and it began to get dark.

The guides said that if they went on, they could reach the village where the chief lived, at about midnight, but that the path to the village was a dangerous one to travel in the dark, since it went through the mountains. The missionary thought for a while. It was dangerous, he knew, but his heart was burning with a desire to tell the chief about Jesus Christ, and so he said, "Let us trust God and go on."

So they continued on their way as the moon rose, giving them light on their path. They walked carefully along the narrow path. On one side the mountain rose up dark and foreboding; on the other side, it dropped off into darkness. Suddenly, they saw a hyena in their path. The Druses who were with the missionary shouted and threw stones at it until it ran away.

They were glad the hyena was gone now, but the Druses said to the missionary that they refused to continue, since it was a saying among their people that "the way a hyena goes is an unlucky way." They wouldn't go another step. Mr. Gobat tried to persuade them to go on, but they refused.

Then the messenger from the chief told the missionary that if they would go back to the village they had just passed, they could sleep there and set out very early the next morning. They would still have time to visit with the chief before heading back to be in time for the ship. That sounded like a good idea to everyone.

But instead of waking up very early, they all overslept because they were so tired. Mr. Gobat was very disappointed. He had wanted to tell the chief about Christ. But he hurried back down the mountain and reached his ship just in time. He felt discouraged at the lost opportunity.

When he reached Malta, he received a letter from a friend in Lebanon, who told him that this chief had no desire at all to hear about the Lord Jesus Christ, but that the whole thing was a plot to kill the missionary. They had planned to lure him to the chief in order to kill him.

But the friend's letter continued. When the chief heard of the wonderful way in which his wicked plan had been overthrown, he was convinced that the God of the missionary was stronger than his gods. This led to the conversion of the chief.

Are not the ways of the Lord wonderful? He has so many ways of keeping His people safe, and of converting sinners to Himself. The Lord protected the missionary, and in this way led the heathen chief to Himself.

"He shall cover thee with his feathers, and under his wings shalt thou trust: his truth shall be thy shield and buckler" (Psalm 91:4).

Question: How did the missionary escape the plot to kill him? What did that escape lead to?
Scripture readings: Psalm 91:3; 2 Timothy 4:18; 2 Peter 2:9.

11. The Russian Servant Girl

Many years ago, an English minister named Rev. Gordon lived in St. Petersburg with his family for several years. The Gordons had several Russian servants working for them. One of these servants was Erena, a bright, intelligent, young woman, who was pleasant and did her work well.

Everything went well until the beginning of Lent, in the spring. Erena was a member of the Greek Orthodox Church. People who attended this church took their religion very seriously. Keeping the fast of Lent was one of their customs, and Erena informed the minister's wife that she wished to attend church twice every day all through Lent. Lent was a period of forty days beginning on Ash Wednesday until Easter. It was a time of penitence, or seeking forgiveness of sin. Sadly, this was mostly done through works, or things the people did, thinking they could gain God's favor in this way.

Erena's mistress told her she did not need to go to church so often, since she was needed to help in the home.

"Do you want me to lose my soul, ma'am?" exclaimed Erena.

"No, far from it," answered Mrs. Gordon.

"I pray for the salvation of your soul. But fasting, and saying prayers, and going to church will not save your soul. There must be something more than all this. The Lord Jesus Christ is the only Savior of sinners, and it is by faith in Him alone that any can be saved."

"Well, that's your religion," replied Erena, "but I have been taught differently. I must follow my own religion."

Mrs. Gordon had taught Erena and the other servants to read, and had given them each a Russian New Testament. One Sunday when the Gordons were getting ready to go to church, Mrs. Gordon asked Erena to take care of the two youngest children in the family. She also asked Erena to please read the tenth chapter of Acts while they were at church.

Erena didn't mind watching the two little children. They played quietly, and Erena found a comfortable chair near the children. Why would Mrs. Gordon want her to read that particular chapter, she wondered. She picked up her Russian New Testament, and quickly found Acts 10. Soon she was absorbed in the story of Cornelius the centurion. When she read about his fasting and praying and giving alms, she was delighted. "This man was of my religion," she thought happily. "He believed in fasting, praying, and giving to the poor."

But when Erena continued reading, she discovered that God sent Peter to Cornelius, who would tell him what he should do (verse 6). Erena was confused. Wasn't his praying and fasting and giving to the poor enough?

As soon as the Gordons returned from church, Erena asked her mistress, "I don't understand. Why did Peter have to speak to Cornelius? Cornelius was a good man. He fasted and prayed and gave money to the poor. Why was it not enough? I was never taught to do anything more."

"Erena," said Mrs. Gordon, "just read the chapter again carefully, and you will find out why the angel was sent to Cornelius."

Erena went to her room and read Acts 10 again. When she came to that beautiful verse, where Peter says, "To him give all the prophets witness, that through his name whosoever believeth in him shall receive remission of sins" (verse 43), she suddenly understood. For the first time in her life she saw clearly how we are to be saved through Jesus. She had been shown the way to heaven. Running downstairs to her mistress, she exclaimed with tears running down her cheeks, "O ma'am, I see it now! I see it now! It was not by fasting that Cornelius the centurion was to be saved; it was not by saying prayers; it was not by giving alms; but it was by believing in Jesus the Son of God. I never saw it before, but I see it now!"

The Holy Spirit had shown Erena the Russian servant girl the way to heaven. It is through Jesus Christ, who said, "I am the way, the truth, and the life: no man cometh unto the Father, but by me" (John 14:6).

Question: Who are we saved through?
Who showed this to Erena?
Scripture reading: Acts 10.

12. A Woman's Kindness is Blessed

L

James and his mother walked hand in hand through the quiet streets of Glasgow, Scotland. It was late Sunday afternoon, and although not all the citizens went to church, the city was quiet.

When they were within sight of the church, James and his mother noticed two young men coming down the street toward them. They were dressed in their work clothes and were unshaven and dirty. They had been drinking. As they passed the church, the young men laughed loudly and began to sing a wicked song. Many of the church people were shocked, and wished that the police would put them in jail.

But Mrs. Allen bent down and whispered to her son, "James, run after those two men and invite them to sit with us in church."

James soon caught up with the two young men and delivered his mother's message. One of them laughed and began to swear, but the other man stopped. He was surprised by the kind invitation. His friend became impatient. "Don't waste your time in church, Will. They're nothing but a bunch of hypocrites." He tried to pull Will along with him. But Will shook him off.

James repeated the invitation, "Come, sit with us, sir. You'd make us very happy if you came along."

Will looked down at James and said, "When I was a boy like you, I went to church every Sunday. I have not been inside a church for three years, and I'm not proud of that. I believe I'll go with you."

James took the man's hand, as if afraid he might change his mind, and led him back to the house of God. Will's friend stood in the street calling curses after him. The boy looked up anxiously at Will, and held his hand more tightly. Will smiled uncomfortably and said, "Some friend, huh?"

James smiled back. "You won't be sorry you came to church, sir. And my mother will be so happy!"

The minister preached from Ecclesiastes 11:1: "Cast thy bread upon the waters: for thou shalt find it after many days." Will listened, but seemed uncomfortable and sad. After church, Will hurried out of church, but Mrs. Allen followed him. "Do you have a Bible, young man?" she asked.

"No ma'am, but I can get one," Will replied.

"Take my son's Bible until you can get one of your own," urged Mrs. Allen. "Read it often during the week, and come again next Sunday. I'll look forward to seeing you."

Will put the Bible in his pocket and hurried away.

At family worship that evening Mrs. Allen prayed earnestly for Will's conversion. During the week she continued to ask God to save the young man.

Next Sunday came, and the next, but Will did not come. Mrs. Allen spoke often of him, and was very sad when he did not come back to church. But on the third Sunday morning, while the congregation was singing the first song, Will entered the Allens' pew. He was neatly dressed, but was thin and pale, as if he had been very sick. Mrs. Allen looked at him with concern, yet she could not hide her smile of thankfulness to see him again.

Immediately after the benediction, Will laid down James's Bible and left the church before James or his mother could catch up with him. Disappointed, they returned to their home. Absently, James leafed through his Bible, then quickly turned back to one of the blank pages in the back. In pencil, Will had written a short note:

"I want to thank you for the interest you have taken in my spiritual welfare. I have been sick, so I could not come to church the last two Sundays. I ask you to remember me in your prayers, as I leave Scotland for my native England in a few days. God bless you both for your kindness to me. W.C."

The years rolled on. Mrs. Allen became sick and passed into her heavenly rest. James grew up to be a doctor, and Will was forgotten.

James was now the medical officer on a ship named the "St. George." This ship was anchored off the coast of South Africa. One evening James was having dinner with some other officers and a doctor-friend whom he hadn't seen for some time.

"Tomorrow is Sunday, James," said Dr. Fielding. "We ought to go to church together in Capetown. It will remind us of old times, when we used to go arm in arm to church in Glasgow."

The next day, James attended church with his friend, Dr. Fielding. After the service, a man who had been sitting behind James asked if he could please look at his Bible. James thought it an odd request, but he handed the man his Bible. The man paged through the Bible and returned it. James turned to go, but the man stopped him.

"Please, sir, could I speak with you for a few moments?" The man appeared to be about thirty-five years old. He was tall and slender and neatly dressed.

"Certainly," answered James, wondering what the man wanted.

James led the man to a bench nearby, and when they were seated the man looked carefully at James.

"You are James Allen," he stated with a smile.

"Yes, I am."

"You lived in Glasgow when you were a boy."

"Yes, I did."

"Did you not once invite a drunken Sabbath-breaker into your church at your mother's request?"

"Yes, I remember that," James answered thoughtfully. Then, suddenly, he understood. "You are Will!" His face lit up and he clapped Will on the back. "My mother never forgot you. She often prayed for you."

"Your mother, is she still alive?" asked Will.

"No," answered James sadly, "she died when I was seventeen years old."

"I am truly sorry to hear it, although I know she is with Jesus now. I would have loved to thank her for inviting a wretch like me into the house of God. She prayed for me, you say?"

Tears glistened in Will's eyes at the thought of Mrs. Allen's kindness and love. In the next half hour James learned Will's story.

Will was born into a happy home where he received a good education and was taught the Word of God. When he was fifteen his father died. It was then Will's responsibility to earn money to support the family. He found a job, but his fellow workers were ungodly men and Will quickly learned their evil ways. He ignored his mother's tears, and hardened his heart against her warnings and pleadings.

He soon left his job and traveled to Scotland where he lived sinfully for two years. "When I left your church that Sunday," confessed Will, "I felt so bad about how I had lived and how I had grieved my mother! I saw you and your mother worshipping God together. It made me think of myself when I was a boy and went to church with my mother and father and sisters.

"I couldn't sleep that Sunday night. I worried so much about my sins that I became sick. I did a lot of thinking and praying and reading in your Bible as I recovered.

"When I got better, I returned to England. I went to the house I grew up in but found that my mother had died." Will bowed his head and shed tears of remorse. "I never thought, when I left home at sixteen, that I'd never see her again. Sin is bitter, James. 'At the last it biteth like a serpent, and stingeth like an adder' (Proverbs. 23:32). God has forgiven me, James, but the consequences of my sin are still painful."

"You have found God's forgiveness? Tell me how God rescued you," prompted James.

"When I found out my mother was dead," continued Will, "I visited my mother's brother. He is also one of God's children. He loved my mother very much, and when I hurt her, I hurt him too. I begged his forgiveness for all the pain I had caused him. He lovingly forgave me. The love of Christ in that man's heart melted my own. I spent some blessed weeks with him. We talked a lot together, we studied God's Word, I sought God's forgiveness, and we rejoiced together in God's forgiving grace.

"I then was led to study for the ministry and became a missionary. I've been here in South Africa for several years. It gives me great joy to work in the service of my loving, gracious Savior.

"The moment I saw your Bible," smiled Will, "I recognized it. That's why I asked you if I could see it. I see the note I wrote to you and your mother is still there.

"So you see, James, how God, by His unfathomable love and boundless grace, used your mother to save me. I was 'a brand plucked out of the fire' (Zechariach. 3:2)."

"I am happy to hear all this," answered James. "I remember that the minister's text that Sunday in Glasgow was from Ecclesiastes 11:1: 'Cast thy bread upon the waters: for thou shalt find it after many days.' That's what has happened with you and me. I now may rejoice because of what God has done. He used my mother's invitation to get you into church and to begin His great work in you. Your story convicts me of my need to be more faithful in His service. So often we doubt God's power, and drag our feet in doing His bidding. What a wonder that God is faithful!"

Question: What animal is sin described as in Proverbs 23:32? How did Ecclesiastes 11:1 come true in James' life?
Scripture reading: Zechariah 3.

13. Carl the Burglar

Carl lived in a large city in Australia many years ago. He had four brothers and two sisters. From the day he was born, Carl was different from the others. He was naughty and difficult, and when he started school, he was always in trouble. Time after time, Carl was expelled from school because he stole from other children.

Worst of all, Carl seemed to have no conscience. If he was punished, he didn't care. He kept on stealing, becoming better at it all the time.

In high school, Carl made friends who encouraged him in his wrong ways. Soon he got into the habit of gambling and drinking. When Carl finished high school, he didn't bother to find a job. He spent his time in the park planning whom he could rob at night. He still lived at home, and he even stole from his family. His family had to make sure their valuables were hidden and locked up. Of course, this caused much grief in Carl's home. The whole family was ashamed of Carl.

Carl didn't care at all that his family was hurt by his wicked life. It was not long before the police were after Carl, and so he left home, ignoring his mother's tears and his father's warnings.

A few days later the police found him and arrested him, but let him go with only a stern warning.

"That was easy!" thought Carl. "If it's always that easy to get away with stealing, I'll try stealing bigger things!"

Within a few weeks, Carl met some people who were professional burglars. They sold what they stole, and this was how they made their money. One of these men owned a tavern where many of the men gambled as they drank. Thieves of the worst kind went in and out of this place day and night. Carl loved it there, and he loved to steal. He enjoyed the excitement and the risk of being caught.

At this tavern, Carl met George, a young man who had been stealing since he was a little boy. Carl and George began doing robberies together.

One of their favorite plans was to go out on a dark night and wait in a quiet place until someone passed. If the person was alone, and if he looked rich, they would rob him. Carl would walk toward the man and ask him if he could tell him the time. In the meantime, George would creep up behind the man and suddenly hit him on the head, knocking him unconscious. Quickly, Carl and George would search the man's pockets, take his watch and rings, and run away. Only once had Carl been frightened, and that was when he thought George might have hit a man too hard and killed him.

On a windy afternoon, George and Carl were walking past a little church in a bad part of town. George interrupted Carl's story about a friend's successful robbery the night before.

"Listen, Carl," he said, pulling him aside. "I want you to give me a hand to steal the organ out of that church."

What a strange thing to steal, you might think! But Carl didn't care what he stole, as long as he had something to steal. It was just another challenge to him. He began to plan with George how they could get the organ out of the church. They had no idea how big the organ was, or what the inside of the church looked like, so they decided it would be best if one of them went to church. On a sign in front of the church it said that there was a men's meeting every Thursday evening.

"I ain't goin' to no church meetin', so you'll be the one goin', Carl," George said.

"I'm not too excited about churches myself," answered Carl, "but if you insist, I'll go."

Thursday evening came, and Carl went to the men's meeting. He was greatly surprised to see many people he used to know: thieves and gamblers. The pastor of the little church was a young man who had been used by the Lord to convert these men and many others who had formerly led wicked lives. The meeting began with singing. Then coffee and cookies were handed out. A few men asked Carl some questions, but Carl was in no mood to be friendly. He had to find a way to steal that organ. Carl felt a bit uncomfortable. He wished he hadn't been so quick to agree to George's ridiculous idea. Besides, he couldn't help wondering what these former thieves found so interesting in this old church.

The minister began his speech. Carl did not listen at first. He settled back in his chair, and tried to figure out through which door they should try and take the organ. But he never finished planning. The minister's words broke into his thoughts and God used them to show Carl what an awful sinner he was. He was so ashamed and alarmed at his wickedness that he fell on his knees and cried to God for mercy.

"I can't say exactly how it happened," Carl explained later to a friend. "I went into that church as a gambler, a drunkard, a thief, and a burglar; the greatest sinner in the city. I came out a changed man. Old things had passed away, and all became new."

So Carl was arrested by the Holy Ghost, who showed him his wicked heart. In due time, God also showed him that He loved His people so much that He sent His only-begotten Son to die instead of them. Carl was always amazed at the great wonder of God's love to such a sinner as he was. He had been serving sin and Satan with all his heart, and God was pleased to stop him and save him from eternal death.

You can imagine how shocked Carl's friends were to hear this news. Carl had planned to do three robberies that week, and of course, now he refused to do them. The police heard of Carl's change, too. They asked the minister if it was true, and warned him that Carl should not be trusted. They thought it was one of Carl's tricks.

The police were wrong. The complete change in Carl's life soon revealed itself in many ways. Carl found a job and worked honestly for his money. Some time later the Lord gave Carl a converted wife. Together they served the Lord, and often spoke to others about the Lord. Carl often went back to his old friends and told them that there is salvation in the Lord Jesus for sinful people. God blessed Carl's efforts, as several of these hardened sinners were also converted.

Question: What did Carl ask God for when he realized he was a sinner? How did he prove the change in his life was real?
Scripture reading: Luke 23:39-43.

14. Caught in the Net!

Several years ago, a minister was sent by God to a fishing village. Most of the villagers went out daily with their boats to fish, except on Sunday, when they went to church.

However, in this village there lived an old fisherman who was, and always had been, very rough and ungodly. He broke the Sabbath, never attended church, cursed those who tried to speak with him about spiritual matters and swore loudly on numerous occasions.

After arriving in this small village, the new minister began visiting all the people with one of his elders. When coming to this old fisherman's house, his elder warned, "If you do not want to hear God's name misused and His Word mocked, do not go there. Speaking with this man about religion is hopeless."

The minister, however, did not agree. He said to his elder, "God opened the eyes of a blind man with clay from the ground. Possibly I am the clay which God plans to use for this old sinner. If he remains hardened, then at least I have done my duty. Let us go; maybe God will bless it."

They both entered the house and saw the gray-haired man sitting on a rough stool, mending a fishing net. He received the men with a stern, cold look, but did not say a word. The minister, being quite a friendly person, asked him questions about fishing – about his nets, his boats, and so on.

Such talk surprised the old fisherman and soon his frown changed into a smile. He liked nothing better than to tell stories about his fishing days and to have people ask him about his experiences at sea. The minister continued this conversation for a full hour and then stood up to leave.

"Come back again – I liked our talk," the old fisherman told the minister. "I like nothing better than talking about fishing."

"I can understand your love for your work," said the minister, "I also love my work. Will you come and listen to me talk about my work next Sunday in church?"

"Never!" the old fisherman responded. "I am not interested in that. I'm a fisherman with body and soul."

"I will promise to speak about fishing, then, if you promise to be in church Sunday morning," the minister replied.

The old man agreed for the minister did seem to have a love for fishing. "But if you start talking about other things, I'll walk out right away!" he threatened.

On Sunday morning, the rough old fisherman was in church – to the amazement of the entire village! The minister preached from Mark 1:16- 18: "Now as He walked by the sea of Galilee, He saw Simon and Andrew his brother casting a net into the sea: for they were fishers. And Jesus said unto them, Come ye after Me, and I will make you to become fishers of men. And straightway they forsook their nets, and followed Him."

With open eyes and ears the old fisherman listened. He never missed a single word. In the application, the minister earnestly warned all sinners to flee to the great Fisher of men, Jesus Christ. God blessed this sermon to the soul of the old fisherman. God's Word broke the hardened heart of this old man. He could not contain himself anymore but cried aloud in the church, "You have caught me in the net!"

The minister paused, and then spoke, "Have I caught you in the net as I desired? May God in His mercy help you out and bring you to liberty!" After that, the old fisherman often went to visit the minister, not to speak about fishing, but about his need for deliverance from sin. God blessed the visits and Jesus Christ became the hope and salvation of this formerly hardened sinner.

Question: Do you value God's messengers and message? How are God's messengers like a fisherman?
Scripture reading: Matthew 4:18-22.

15. Covey's Loss and Gain

Covey was a sailor and he loved it. As a boy, he would study his father's books about ships, imagining himself as a strong, courageous sailor aboard one of these fine vessels. Not once did he imagine that he would be badly injured on a ship, but it actually happened. He lost both legs in a battle at sea. The doctor had sad news for him now. "We will have to amputate still further, Covey."

The sailor swore. "I guess your scissors will have to finish what the cannonball started."

"I'm afraid so, my brave fellow," replied the doctor.

"Well, never mind," said Covey. "I may have lost both my legs, and maybe I'll lose my life too, but," he continued, with a terrible curse, "we have to beat the Dutch, we have to beat the Dutch!"

Covey was a good sailor, for he was never afraid of danger. But neither was he afraid of sin. About two weeks before the battle between the English and the Dutch, Covey had dreamed that they were fighting when suddenly both his legs were shot away, and that he lost his mind. This dream frightened him so much that he thought he should try to pray. But he did not like to pray because he did not like to think about God. His conscience told him God was angry with him. Covey thought he could push these gloomy thoughts away by drinking and blaspheming with the other sailors. But he just couldn't get these thoughts out of his head. Day and night he had thoughts of God, hell and death. Soon, however, the sight of the Dutch ships and the sailors' talk of the brave deeds they planned to do drove these thoughts away.

When the time of the battle drew near, the noble Admiral ordered his men to lie flat on the deck. In this way he hoped to save the lives of the sailors. When the Dutch were close enough, they would be able to aim better, the Admiral figured. By now the hard-hearted, wicked Covey had lost all his fears of a few days before. He cursed and swore at the sailors who were lying on the deck. Covey did not want to obey the Admiral's orders, but when he saw an officer near him, he did not dare to disobey, so he leaned over the barrel which stood close to him and waited until the command was given to shoot at the Dutch ships. He wanted to prove that he was not afraid!

Finally the command to shoot was shouted out. The same instant that Covey stood up, a cannonball tore away one of his legs and most of the other one. It all happened so quickly that he did not realize until he fell to the deck.

After the doctor had amputated what was left of his legs, he thought about his dream. He said to himself, "If the first part of my dream came true, the rest of it will probably come true, too." He became so afraid of this that it is a wonder that he did not lose his mind.

Some time later Covey was discharged from the Haslar Hospital. He walked with the help of two wooden legs and two crutches. He was very troubled, for he feared that God would be just in taking away not only his legs, but also his mind and soul.

The following Sunday evening Covey went to Orange Street Chapel in Portsea. The minister's text was on Mark 5:15: "And they come to Jesus, and see him that was possessed with the devil, and had the legion, sitting, and clothed, and in his right mind." The minister explained that this man was a picture of all sinners. But the man sitting at the feet of Jesus after he had been healed was a picture of a sinner converted to God by the gospel, enjoying peace of mind, and receiving instruction from Jesus, the friend of sinners.

Covey listened in surprise. "I wonder who told the minister all about me? How did he know I was going to be in church tonight? Why would he make a sermon all about me, a poor, wooden-legged sailor?" He just did not understand it. His sins came to his memory, and filled him with horror. For a few minutes he was filled with despair. He thought he would die and be lost. But then he heard the minister saying that Jesus Christ was just as willing to save the most wicked sinner as He was to save the man possessed with a devil. He said that a person was also restored to his right mind when he believed in Jesus.

Suddenly Covey understood his dream. He had been spiritually out of his mind all of his life. If he would love and serve the Lord Jesus, he would come to his senses. Now he was overjoyed. As he heard about Jesus' amazing love to sinners, Covey's despair and horror turned into hope and joy. Jesus died to save wicked sinners!

A few weeks after this, Covey visited the pastor. Covey told him about his life as a sailor, but also about his first Sunday in church. What a surprise it was when the minister said he hadn't known Covey before this visit, nor did he preach that sermon because of Covey, even though it had been the very sermon Covey had needed to hear. About a year later, Covey joined the church.

The years passed, and the time came for Covey to die. The minister visited Covey when he heard of his illness. When the pastor entered the room, Covey exclaimed, "Come in, thou man of God! I have been hoping you'd come so I could tell you how happy I am. I think I will soon die, but death does not frighten me. 'The sting of death is sin... But thanks be to God, which giveth us the victory through our Lord Jesus Christ.'

(1 Corinthians 15:56-57) I am going to heaven! Oh, what Jesus has done for me, 'the chief of sinners'! (1 Timothy 1:15)

"I used to think it must be difficult to die, but now I find it easy. I am glad because of God's love. I will soon be rid of my sinful heart. I will be with God forever! My thoughts of God, of myself, and of eternity are so different now from when I lost my legs on the ship. What a precious loss that was to me! Oh my dear minister, after I die, please preach a sermon for a poor sailor? Tell others, especially sailors, who are as ignorant and wicked as I was, that poor, blaspheming Covey found mercy with God through faith in the blood of Christ. Tell them that if I found mercy, no one who seeks it need despair. You know better than I do what to say to them, of course; but be earnest and plead with them. May the Lord grant that my wicked neighbors and fellow sailors may find mercy as well as Covey."

He said much more, but soon his Lord called him to Himself. The last words he uttered as he went through the heavenly gates were, "Hallelujah! Hallelujah!"

Question: What are Christians delivered from when they arrive in heaven with the Lord?
Scripture reading: Mark 5:1-20.

16. God Stops a Sailor

Jerry Creed was born in 1753 near Gravesend, England. His parents paid little attention to Jerry, so he learned early in life to fend for himself.

Ever since Jerry was a little boy, he dreamed of becoming a sailor. He wanted to escape his unhappy life by seeking adventure on the seas. At last he got a job on a ship named *The Marquis of Rockingham*. He was going to be a sailor. And he was on his way to India!

But the voyage did not go as planned. The ship was wrecked on the Malabar Coast (south-western coast of India), leaving Jerry with only the clothes he was wearing. He made his way, about four hundred miles across India, begging as he went, until he came to a port city occupied by the British. There he entered the British Navy. It was very dangerous, but it was his only option. He fought in many intense battles, but God protected Jerry, although Jerry never asked God for His help. Fellow soldiers fell in great numbers all around him, causing Jerry to boast of his "good luck." Over the next few years, he bragged to the other sailors about his many narrow escapes, never giving thanks to God who had spared him so remarkably.

When Jerry tired of a seafaring life, he left the service and returned to Gravesend, where he married and bought a small cottage. He earned his living as a boatman, which means he operated a boat, bringing people and goods to various places along the river.

Jerry was always a bad man, but now he became worse than ever, so that he became known as "wicked Jerry Creed." He cursed and swore in every sentence he uttered. He was a drunkard, and when he drank he became violent. He treated his wife shamefully. His heart was full of enmity against God, and he hated God's people.

Once, when Jerry was on a boat, some Christian passengers began to sing a hymn of praise to God. It made Jerry so angry that he tried to drown out their singing by cursing them and himself as loudly as he could. The passengers ignored him. Jerry, still cursing and blaspheming God, got off the boat as quickly as possible.

The apostle Paul says in 1 Timothy 1:13: "[I] who was before a blasphemer, and a persecutor, and injurious: but I obtained mercy." Jerry Creed was a blasphemer. He was an enemy of God and His people. But he found mercy.

Jerry was drunk the evening he stumbled into a small shop. He needed to buy some supplies. While he waited for the shopkeeper to wrap the supplies, he was cursing and swearing. The shopkeeper shook his head sadly. He felt sorry for this unhappy man and wanted to help him. He knew it would be useless to try to talk to Jerry when he was so drunk, but he had an idea. He took a copy of the story of "Covey the Sailor" and tucked it into Jerry's coat pocket. "My friend," said the shopkeeper, "you seem to be a wholesale dealer in sin. Read this little book in the morning, if God spares you."

Jerry did not remember how he got home that night, but he did remember the shopkeeper. He took the little book out of his pocket and read it. While he read, the Spirit of God opened his heart to receive the truth. Before Covey was converted, he was very much like Jerry Creed. Jerry read the little story several times. The more he read it, the more he felt convinced that he was living in a state of awful rebellion against God. And then Jerry did something he never dreamed he would do: He began to pray for mercy!

The very next Sunday Jerry went to church. He couldn't remember ever having been to church, but he felt he had to go. It was, however, not easy. Jerry had fought many battles as a brave sailor, but taking the first step in the ways of God was the hardest thing he had ever done. He was afraid the people would not welcome him since he had been so cruel to these very people. Satan did his best to keep Jerry from God and His Word, but God was stronger!

Slowly, Jerry approached the church. He didn't dare to go in. He was so ashamed of himself! He didn't deserve mercy. He waited until the service had started, then stepped inside the door, but did not enter the sanctuary. That way he could listen to the sermon but no one would notice him.

Jerry did this for several weeks. Finally, one Sunday he entered the sanctuary and sat in the back pew. He sat with his elbows on the pew in front of him, supporting his head with his hands, keeping his eyes fixed on the minister. Under the power of the Word big tears trembled in his eyes, which he dashed away, but they were soon followed by other tears which rolled down his weather-beaten cheeks.

These were the tears of repentance. He felt that he had sinned against a kind and merciful Father. He wondered at the patience of God toward him, a vile blasphemer. Now, when he recalled his narrow escapes, he marveled at God's protecting grace.

Jerry continued going to church. He learned about the way of salvation. In the Lord Jesus Christ, he found the Friend he needed — One willing and able to save to the uttermost. Jerry was led to cry out, "Lord, save me, a poor, lost sinner!" The following hymn describes Jerry's hope in Jesus alone to save him:

Jesus, to Thee alone I fly,
And wilt Thou let a sinner die
Whilst trusting in Thy sacred blood?
I seek no other way to God.

Thy tender heart will surely forgive,
And bid a trembling sinner live;
For all that come, Thy grace is free,
For Saul, and Magdalene, and me!

Jerry Creed was a changed man, for he became a new creature in Christ (2 Corinthians. 5:17). He faithfully attended church, and prayer meetings. He refused to work on the Sabbath even though he used to make more money on Sundays than all the rest of the days of the week together. Jerry willingly gave up the extra money in order to keep the Sabbath day holy.

When Jerry was sixty-six years old, he was not strong enough to work much anymore. But God provided: "Seek ye first the kingdom of God and his righteousness; and all these things shall be added unto you" (Matthew 6:33). A relative passed away, leaving Jerry with enough money to live comfortably with his wife till his death.

Jerry became meek and gentle, meeting the scorn of his friends with kindness and patience. Never once was he heard to speak angrily or foolishly. The behavior of his former friends reminded him of his own behavior before God saved him. He would talk to them and invite them to church, hoping and praying for their salvation. Even those who hated him had to admit that Jerry was a changed man.

Jerry was a true Christian, called from death to life in Christ. Every act of his life testified that he had been "called out of darkness into his marvelous light" (1 Peter. 2:9). The longer he lived, the closer was his walk with God.

On the evening before he died, Jerry went to church, though he had some trouble breathing. Before the sun rose the next morning, Jerry Creed was brought unto his desired haven (Psalm 107:30). On his grave stone above his name is inscribed: "BUT I OBTAINED MERCY."

Question: What awful things did both Paul and Jerry do before they came to know the Lord Jesus Christ?
Scripture reading: Acts 26:12-32.

17. Jack Robbins, the Sailor

Mr. Taylor always enjoyed his ten-minute walk home from work. He often saw the same people, also walking home after a long day at work. Sometimes he saw unfamiliar faces. Today he noticed an English sailor hobbling over the pavement as well as he could with his wooden leg and his crutch. The sailor kept looking at Mr. Taylor as though he wanted to speak with him. When he came near, he pulled off his hat and shook Mr. Taylor's hand, with tears streaming down his face. Mr. Taylor was a little confused by this unusual behavior. Finally the sailor asked, "Don't you remember me, sir?"

Mr. Taylor thought the man looked familiar, but he could not remember his name. He shook his head. "I'm sorry, I can't remember."

"Jack Robbins, sir," the sailor introduced himself.

Suddenly Mr. Taylor remembered. Jack Robbins had been in his Sunday school class about twenty years ago. He had certainly changed! He had lost one of his legs and an eye. His face was badly scarred. "What! Jack, is it really you?"

"Yes, it is the same Jack Robbins. I've thought about you and your kind warnings many times since then; I will never forget my Sunday school teacher."

"I'm very glad to see you, Jack," said Mr. Taylor. "I'm on my way home now. Why don't you come and have supper with my wife and me? I'd love to hear your story."

Jack agreed, and as soon as supper was finished, the three of them sat around the fire, and Jack began his interesting story.

"How long is it now that you've been gone?" asked Mrs. Taylor.

"Last month it was nineteen years ago, ma'am," answered the sailor. "I remember the day very well. You visited me the evening before I left for sea, Mr. Taylor. You warned me about the temptations I would face, and you prayed for me, too. You prayed that I would be kept from temptations, and that I would be led to think seriously about the instructions I had received in Sunday school, even though I would be far away from home and church. I was a reckless young man, and you asked God to show me the danger I was in. Then you committed me to the care of the Almighty God and prayed for my salvation.

"You gave me a pocket Bible, and told me to read it every day. I still have that Bible. Here it is." He pulled it out of his pocket and handed it to Mr. Taylor.

Mr. Taylor opened it and recognised his handwriting in the front: "*John Taylor presents this Bible to Jack Robbins, hoping that he will read it prayerfully when he is far from home, and that he will treasure its truths in his heart and live in obedience to it."*

"Now I remember," said Mr. Taylor. "You were in my class for a few years in a row, weren't you?"

"Yes, sir, but what I learned from you was not enforced at home, so that any impressions I did have quickly wore off. When I was about fifteen I quit school because I didn't like the strict rules they had. I wanted freedom. I roamed the streets with a few other boys, and when they decided to go to sea I said I'd go with them.

"It wasn't hard to find a place on a ship. Once aboard though, I found temptations all around me. There was no Sunday school teacher to warn me, and I never read my Bible. I joined other sailors in their rough lifestyle, and soon I was as bad as they were.

"I had imagined that being a sailor would be lots of fun, but it was hard work. Besides, the captain had strict rules and we didn't dare to disobey him. Even though I seemed hardened, my conscience bothered me sometimes. I knew I would have no excuse in the great Judgment Day, for I had been to Sunday school for five years, and I had a Bible. Sometimes a verse from the Bible that I had memorized before came back and bothered me for a while. It was the first Sunday on the ship, and I was playing cards with the others. I knew it was wrong, but I didn't dare to be different. I couldn't concentrate on the game because this text kept pounding in my head: 'The wicked are like the troubled sea when it cannot rest, whose waters cast up mire and dirt. There is no peace, saith my God, to the wicked.' (Isaiah 57:20-21) But instead of listening to God's Word, I ignored it and refused to repent. I cursed and swore louder than the others, and often I was drunk.

"After seven years, I went home for a visit. During these seven years I had had many narrow escapes from death, but God had been pleased to spare my life. When I came home, I found that my father had died about six months before, and my mother was very sick, with no money to pay the doctor. I was glad I could help her. I took care of her and made sure she got the medicines she needed to get well again.

"I wanted very badly to see you before I went back to sea, but I knew you would not be happy with my sinful life, so I didn't go. But two weeks before I had to leave, I met William Adams who had been in my Sunday school class. He told you that I was in town, and you came to see me the very next day. The very sight of you was like a dagger in my heart. You tried to talk seriously with me, but I purposely changed the subject every time. Then you prayed with me, but I did not want to listen to that either. I remember you had tears in your eyes as you handed me some tracts and some good books. You told me to read them carefully and to think about eternity. Do you remember that, Mr. Taylor?"

"Yes, Jack, I remember it. The next Sunday I told the children about the danger of ignoring the Word of God, and of having wicked friends. I used you as an example. I told them that you were a nice boy when you were young, and that you enjoyed coming to Sunday school, but that you had become a very wicked man who would not listen to the words of the Lord anymore. The children were very impressed by this example. At the end of the lesson we prayed together for 'poor Jack Robbins, the wicked sailor.' I asked God to keep the children from following his bad example, and to give also Jack Robbins a new heart. If I am not mistaken, I think the Lord has answered that prayer."

"I will always be thankful for you and your prayers, Mr. Taylor. Sometimes it is a long time before God answers the prayers of His people, but He never forgets them. His time is always the best time.

"When I returned to the ship I felt ashamed of my behavior towards you. I thought I should read the tracts you had given me. I was such a wicked person, Mr. Taylor, that I often used to make jokes about the serious things I read, just so that I could have a good laugh. But even while I was laughing, my conscience accused me. I was not happy, but instead of turning to the Lord, I blamed you for teaching me from the Bible. If I had never heard your warnings, my conscience wouldn't bother me, and I could enjoy myself, I thought.

"There was a new sailor on this ship. His name was Isaac North. He made things even worse for me because he carried on with the warnings where you left off. He refused to join us in our ungodly games and jokes. We made fun of him and nicknamed him 'Preacher North' because he was always reading his Bible. Our captain used to say that he wished we were all religious if that meant we would be as diligent and willing to work as Isaac North was.

"Once Isaac was in my cabin to ask me about a task I had just finished, when he saw my Bible. He opened it and read what you had written in the front. He asked all about you and what you had taught me in Sunday school. Then he noticed the books and tracts, and asked if he could read them. He took one at a time, and every time he returned it, he warned me to pay attention to what I had learned. Once he said to me, 'Jack, if a religious boy becomes a wicked man, he is ten thousand times more guilty than a boy who has never heard about the Lord Jesus, "for unto whomsoever much is given, of him shall be much required."' (Luke 12:48)

"I liked Isaac, but I would never admit it to anyone. I often wished I dared to be like him. He was always cheerful, even though we teased him a lot. I listened to Isaac when we were alone, but if another sailor was around, I made fun of his warnings.

"I am ashamed to say that the Lord had to use stronger measures to break my rebellion. We were fighting one of the enemy's ships, when Henry Brown was hit. He was the most wicked of us all. His shoulder was badly wounded and one of his legs was torn off. We won that battle. I went to see Henry afterwards, and knew immediately that his life was in danger. When he saw me he said, 'Jack, listen to me. I am lost forever! My sins bother me more than my pain. I have nowhere to go. I have no hope! I am lost forever!' I felt awful. I couldn't comfort him because I knew I was no better than he was. I ran and got Isaac North. Henry had treated Isaac cruelly, but Isaac was glad to be able to talk to Henry. He tried to tell him about the Lord Jesus who also saved the thief on the cross, but Henry kept moaning, 'There is no mercy for me. There is only darkness for me.' Isaac tried to pray with him, but Henry stopped him. 'I have cursed and blasphemed God all my life. He will not hear me now. It's too late. I already feel the anger of the Lord.' Soon after this he slipped into a coma. I was sitting at his bedside when he died a few hours later. I was deeply impressed. 'It could have been me,' I thought. 'If I had died instead of Henry, how terrible my end would have been. I would now be in hell with no hope of mercy.'

"When I got back to my room and picked up my jacket from the bed, I noticed that it had been shot through in two places. My hat had a bullet hole in it too. That really made me think. God had spared me when death had come so close. I began to think about my sinful life. I had been so rebellious against the Lord who had been patient for so many years. I felt no one had ever committed so many sins as I had, and I thought there could be no mercy for me either. I didn't play games or drink with the others anymore. I thought it was all so disgusting. Isaac noticed that I was more quiet and he tried to talk with me as often as he could. I told him exactly how I was feeling. I believe the Lord has blessed these conversations to my heart. The Lord enabled me to flee with all my sins and guilt to Him, trusting in His finished work on the Cross. I experienced that the Lord had cast all my sins into the depth of the sea. Then I loved to read the Bible and the books you had given me. I've learned a lot from them.

"About a month after this we fought against another French ship and just before we captured it, I got these scars on my face and lost one of my eyes; I was shot in the face. They didn't think I'd live, but God spared me once again.

"I've fought in eleven battles, and I've

been shipwrecked twice, but God has been pleased to spare me until now.

"Two years ago while we were fighting in Trafalgar, Isaac was wounded. He died a few days later, but he died trusting in his Savior to the end.

"About eighteen months ago I lost my leg by a cannon shot. Happily, we were close to England, and they were able to get me to the hospital in time. My leg was amputated, but everything went well and I feel as healthy as I ever did."

Tears of joy flowed that evening as Jack told his story, humbly acknowledging God's goodness in his life. Before Jack left, Mr. Taylor thanked God for bringing back a wandering sheep into His fold.

Question: Who is more guilty than a sinner who has not heard about Christ? Read Haggai 1:12 & 13. When the people had repented, what words does God use to comfort them?
Scripture Reading: Psalm 107:17-32.

18. Jorgan's Raccoon

Jorgan Scheuler lived in a log cabin in the Rocky Mountains. His father and brothers did not care for religion. Ever since his mother died, Jorgan was raised without hearing the Bible read. He grew up learning to fight, drink, and swear. He never thought about those things which are good.

Jorgan's family depended on hunting and fishing for their food. They hunted for deer, wild turkeys and raccoons. One Sunday night, Jorgan went hunting with his three brothers. The moon was full as they entered the forest. Before long, George, his oldest brother, whispered, "Look! There's a big raccoon up in that tall tree."

"But we can never get that one!" answered Ernest quietly, "That raccoon is up way too high." The boys did not have a gun, so someone would have to climb the tree to shake the raccoon down.

"Wait!" Jorgan whispered, "I can climb almost as well as any raccoon. I'll climb that tree. We can't miss a big one like that!"

Jorgan began climbing, with his eye on the branch where the raccoon was hiding. Higher and higher he climbed until at last he was level with the branch. The raccoon began to back up going farther and farther out on the limb. Jorgan carefully climbed onto the branch, giving it a shake. But the raccoon still hung on. Carefully, Jorgan inched his way closer, shaking the branch as he went. But his shaking was not enough to knock the raccoon down. With all his might, Jorgan gave one more hard shake. But in the next instant, the branch broke and he was falling down, down, down.

Terrified, Jorgan cried out, "Lord, have mercy on me!"

As soon as the cry left his lips, Jorgan's hands caught hold of a branch. There he hung, still high in the tree, with no more branches under him. He felt as though he hung between heaven and hell. "If I let go of this branch," he thought, "I will fall straight down into hell!" In vain he struggled to climb back on the branch. Again he cried out, "Lord, have mercy on me!" He received strength to climb back on the limb, and was then able to slowly climb back down the tree. When he reached the ground, he was too weak to stand. George and Ernest helped their shaken brother walk home. They put him to bed.

But Jorgan could not sleep that night. What terrible thoughts filled his mind! "What if the branch I caught had broken? The devil would have me now. I would be burning in hell!" Jorgan tossed and turned all night with terrible thoughts filling his head.

Jorgan went to work the next morning as

usual. But he could not laugh and swear as he usually did. What a burden he had to carry! "What's the matter, Jorgan? You look so sad. Are you sick?"

Jorgan thought to himself, "Yes, I am sick. But sin is the cause of it." He did not know what to do. He had never prayed except when he hung helpless in the tree. He had no Bible and he had never heard a minister preach. "I must find a Bible," he thought, "and I must find a minister."

Jorgan remembered that his mother's Bible was hidden in an old trunk. She had died when Jorgan was still a child, and in anger, Jorgan's father had put her Bible away. Now Jorgan sneaked into the cabin and found it. He began to read the Bible every spare minute that he had. But the more he read, the heavier his burden became. He saw hell and punishment in everything he read. He read that the wicked would burn in hell and that there was no peace for the wicked forever. Jorgan knew he was very wicked. He felt that all these curses were on his head. How miserable he became! "If the Bible does not take away my sin, whatever can I do?" he sighed.

Jorgan began to escape to the woods where he would fall down on his knees behind a tree. He tried to pray, but didn't know what to pray. He no longer wanted to be with his brothers and friends. It made him feel terrible to hear them laughing and swearing. He tried to escape by working on the opposite side of the field. Whenever he could, Jorgan would go into the woods to pray. "Jorgan's head is all mixed up," his brothers would say. "It happened when he fell from the tree."

Although Jorgan still tried to read the Bible and pray, he only became more miserable. Every day he read and read, but one day he became so miserable that he thought he would surely die. Yet he knew that he had to continue reading the Bible, even though he only saw hell before his eyes. That day, however, when he began to read, he suddenly read about Jesus. He saw that Jesus could stand between him and his sins. What a joy filled his heart! There was a possibility for salvation in Jesus Christ for a sinner like him.

A new love for Jesus filled Jorgan's heart. He could not wait to share the wonderful news with his brothers. He ran to the field to share his wonderful experience, but his brothers only laughed at him. They had never seen their sins. They did not feel their need for the Lord Jesus. "Jorgan," they replied, "your mind is still mixed up. You don't know what you are talking about."

Years later, Jorgan was working as a blacksmith in a nearby town and he saw Reverend Morris ride past on his horse. Excitedly, Jorgan mounted his own horse and rode after the minister. "Reverend! Please stop. I must speak with you."

Reverend Morris stopped and waited

for Jorgan to catch up. Without introducing himself, Jorgan began speaking rapidly. "Oh Reverend! I have waited for years to speak to a minister of God's Word. I have longed to tell what has happened in my soul. Come to my cabin so I may tell you about it."

When Reverend Morris saw the woods, he hesitated. But when he saw how sincere Jorgan was, he followed him. Soon they reached the rough log cabin that was Jorgan's home. With tears of thankfulness streaming down his face, Jorgan told of the misery and struggles he had experienced, but also of how he had found Jesus in the Bible. He shared his great joy in seeing Jesus stand between God and his sins.

Reverend Morris was impressed by Jorgan's conversion. He saw that Jorgan's only teacher was the Spirit of God who had applied the Bible to his heart. No minister had been necessary for his conversion. He saw that awakened sinners all experience the same thing—misery, deliverance, and thankfulness. Jorgan had felt his burden of sin; he had turned to the Bible for salvation and deliverance, and he had returned to God in thanksgiving. But above all, Jorgan's conversion shows the gracious care of the Great Shepherd, Jesus Christ, for His sheep.

Question: Who was Jorgan's only teacher?
In Nahum 1:7, what do we learn about God?
Scripture reading: Psalm 51.

19. Judgment and Warning

Towards the end of a warm summer evening some three hundred years ago, an old-fashioned coach made its way up a steep road in Scotland. The horse-drawn carriage contained two travelers. One was a young man, and the other was a kindly middle-aged gentleman. Judging by his clothes, it was clear that he was a minister.

A little further lay the town of Dunblane, where the pastor planned to preach the next day. Inside the coach, the young man was listening closely to a story the minister was telling about God's ways with His people.

The story was cut short by a loud cry which shattered the stillness of the evening.

"Shh, Henry!" exclaimed the minister in a loud whisper. "What was that noise? Stop the horses a minute and I'll go and see what's going on." The minister climbed out of the coach and looked around. They had reached a crossroad, and a little way down the side road the minister saw a very excited man pointing to what looked like a person lying on the ground.

"Stop! Stop!" cried the man, wringing his hands. "For pity's sake, help me!"

The minister acted quickly. "Wait here till I get back, Henry. I'm going to see what's wrong." He ran over to the man without waiting for Henry's reply.

The man immediately began thanking the minister for his kindness. He was a tall, muscular man. His worn, mud-spattered shoes, and sturdy walking stick indicated that he had already traveled quite some distance. "Thank you, sir, oh thank you for taking pity on a poor fellow in trouble. It's very kind of you to help out."

But the minister had no time to listen to thanks. He turned his attention to the man on the ground. The deathly pale face was smeared with dirt, and the afflicted man writhed in apparent pain.

"What's the matter?" asked the pastor, concern in his voice.

"Oh sir, I've had the fright of my life!" answered the man. "My friend here suddenly dropped to the ground. I think he's dying!"

Just then the man on the ground gasped and struggled as if he were exhausted.

"Let's move him to the carriage," suggested the minister, bending over the unfortunate man. But as he did so, the man who had shouted for help roughly grabbed the unsuspecting pastor. The dying man suddenly became very much alive, brandishing a pistol which he had hidden underneath him. The man who had so profusely thanked the minister now cruelly laughed at him. "Alright, hand over your wallet, and be quick about it."

"Yeah, hurry up," added his friend. "It's time for my funeral and I need money for a coffin." He laughed harshly at his offensive remark and pushed the pistol into the minister's back.

For a moment the pastor's face reflected painful surprise, but seeing resistance was useless, he allowed them to search his pockets, all the while praying for God's protection. Calmly he spoke to the thieves. "My friends, stolen money carries a curse with it. Your ill-timed happiness will end in sorrow. I warn you, change your ways before it is too late."

One of the men seemed somewhat stirred in his conscience by this sincere admonition. But his companion who had played the dying man, was entirely unmoved. "Cut out the preachin', wise guy. We want your money, not your sermons. Now get going and don't you dare breathe a word of this to anyone, or we'll take care you never preach again."

The penniless preacher strode back to the waiting coach.

"I saw everything," whispered Henry, "but I thought it would make things worse if I tried to rescue you."

"I'm glad you didn't try to rescue me, Henry. Those men would probably have shot us both if you did. But what a shameful set up, to imitate death as a means of achieving their goal. It pains me to see them pursuing their wicked aims. Often they are ruined by these very goals. These thieves are more hardened than most, I believe."

By this time they had almost reached the top of the hill, and in the valley they could see the church steeple of Dunblane shimmering in the crimson glow of the setting sun. Just at that moment, however, the same cry which had interrupted their journey before, was heard again. Soon the same man came running up to the coach.

"Oh stop, sir!" he shouted. "Please believe me!" he continued in a terror-stricken voice. "It's really true this time. My friend really is dead. Please stop and help me!"

"Ha! You just want to rob me now," jeered Henry. "Be satisfied with what you already have. We're almost in Dunblane, and we're telling the police right away."

"Oh no, sir! I'm serious! Honest, I am! I wouldn't risk being caught in this way if I weren't!" The man was so obviously terrified that the travelers thought he must be a very good actor if this was not real fear. After a moment's hesitation, the carriage came to a halt.

"What's the matter this time?" demanded the minister.

"Oh, sir, please come back! The man whom you saw on the ground really is dead this time. He died right after you left. Oh, please come back with me!" He looked anxiously from one traveler to the other as he wiped the perspiration from his damp forehead.

"Perhaps you think I'm easily deceived, Henry, but I'm quite sure that he's telling the truth. I'd like to see this strange adventure to its end. If you'd rather stay here, I'll go on alone."

"No, I'm going with you, no matter what," stated Henry firmly.

So they returned to the site of the robbery, where they soon discovered that the man was not lying. The body of the robber who had been feigning death lay on the road, his face visibly stamped by the king of terrors. As the minister knelt down to see if he could possibly revive the man, he was struck with awe at the reality of this death. The exact cause of death was unknown to him, but there was no doubt that he was beyond assistance. He had been summoned into eternity almost at the very moment of committing his crime.

"This is a fearful warning, my friend," said the minister, turning to the surviving robber. The thief, forgetful of the fact that he could easily have been arrested by the travlers, seemed confused and overwhelmed by this shocking experience. "These are the bitter fruits of the life that you are leading."

The robber lowered his gaze under the pastor's intent look. "Take back your money, sir," he stammered, holding out the stolen wallet. "And believe me, I'll never again steal a penny as long as I live."

"Don't trust your own resolutions, my friend," replied the minister. "You must ask the Lord, who has so clearly shown you His power, to enable you to lead an honest life from now on. Here is something to get you started," he added, pressing some money into the man's still trembling hands. "I hope you will soon find yourself a good job."

"Thank you, sir! You are very kind to me," he said softly, and this time his thanks were sincere.

Question: Why should we not trust in our own resolutions? What does Habakkuk ask God to do towards the end of the verse Habakkuk 3:2?
Scripture reading: Psalm 34:11-22.

20. "Mary, I Love You Still"

At last Mary was allowed to move from her cottage home in the country to a large city nearby. Her father was dead, and her mother had not wanted to part with her. "How can I let you live among strangers in a place where there are so many temptations, and no one to give you advice?" she asked Mary.

The poor widow finally agreed, however, and Mary left the home of her childhood. At first, the weekly letters exchanged were warm and loving. The loving mother eagerly anticipated each letter. She cherished every word, even the little things about clothes and friends, for she was deeply concerned about her daughter.

As time went on, however, she noticed that Mary's letters were changing. Mary no longer asked for advice, and was not sharing much about her life. The letters gradually became shorter and less loving, and finally stopped arriving altogether.

The poor widow's heart sank, and in her trouble she cast her burden upon her "Burden-bearer," the Lord Jesus Christ. Day after day she prayed that He would guide and protect her daughter.

Then sad news reached the mother's ears from the distant city—news that nearly broke her heart. She heard that her daughter had forgotten her loving words of warning and advice, had forgotten her mother's God, and had so far forgotten herself that she was leading a life of sin and shame. When the mother heard this, she decided to find her lost child. She at once set out for the city and upon arriving there, began to look for the place where her daughter was living. This was difficult, for she had moved from the address where her mother had sent her letters. Day and night, into every likely place, the poor heart-broken mother went in search of her wandering child.

After a number of days of searching without success, she decided to return home, but a new thought flashed across her mind. She went to the photographer's and had her picture taken. She had a number of copies made and then went to the various places of sin, asking permission to hang them on the walls. It was a strange request, indeed, but seeing the type of person she was, no one turned her away.

Some time after that, the daughter and her friend walked into one of these places. Her attention was immediately drawn to the picture on the wall. She said, "That looks like my mother!" She went to look at it more closely, and exclaimed in amazement, "It is my mother!" Then she noticed something written at the bottom, and recognized the familiar handwriting at once. But she was not prepared for what those words expressed: "Mary, I love you still!"

This was too much for her. She was prepared for scoldings and hard words, and expected nothing else. But to think that her mother had actually been searching for her in these places of sin and folly, and was willing to receive her back home just as she was, she could not understand. As she thought about the words, "Mary, I love you still!" the days of her childhood came back before her and all the memories of her godly home – her mother's prayers, tears, and loving advice. As she thought about the difference between what she was then and what she was now, she broke down. Tears flowed as her heart broke. The awfulness of her evil ways was clearly brought into her mind, and she at once decided to leave her sinful friends to go back to her mother. Great was the joy of the widowed mother at the unexpected arrival of her long-lost daughter.

Question: This story pictures God's sincere invitation for sinners to repent and return unto Him. Can you see how this story compares with the story of the prodigal son? Read Hosea 14. In verse 4 what does God promise to heal when the people repent and turn back to Him?
Scripture reading: Luke 15:11-32.

21. Mary and Her Father

About three miles outside a lovely village was a little farm where there once lived a man named John Linn. He was a wicked man. He drank, swore, and was mean. Some of his children grew up to be just like him. They moved away and began lives of their own. Only the youngest little girl was left at home, and that was Mary.

Life on the farm with her father was very unpleasant. She had no mother, and her father ignored her, or else demanded that she work hard.

A kind lady in the village felt sorry for Mary, and persuaded her father to let the girl go and live with her. Mrs. Kent took good care of Mary. She sent her to school and on Sundays she took her to Sunday school and church. After a short time, Mary came to know and love the Lord Jesus, and she became a humble, happy Christian.

Not long after Mary became a Christian, a minister visited the village, and he talked so earnestly to sinners, and urged them so tenderly to come to the Savior, that Mary kept saying to herself, "Oh, if only my poor father could hear this man preach!"

The more she thought of it, the more she was convinced that if her father could only be brought to hear the gospel, he would be converted and turn from being a wicked, drunken, profane man to being a meek and humble child of God.

Mary could not rest until she had seen her father. Her heart was filled with constant prayer to God, pleading for his conversion.

Later the next day Mary set out to visit her father. It was bitterly cold, and the snow lay deep upon the frozen ground. She had to walk three long miles to reach the farm, but Mary's love for her father warmed her heart as she ploughed through the snow, lifting up her heart in prayer to God that her visit would be blessed.

This was no small task Mary was doing. She was actually afraid of her father. Never had she run to him and hugged him, or climbed on his lap to sit with him. She had never even seen him smile before. Mary knew that her father had not been to church in years, and that only God's grace could make him willing to go.

When Mary finally arrived at the farm, cold and tired, she found her father in the barn. She got right to the reason of her visit before she lost her courage. "Daddy, I have come to ask you to go to church with me this evening. We have a visiting minister who is preaching for us this week, and I would be so happy if you would come to hear him. Will you come with me?"

John Linn looked at Mary as though she were crazy. "Me? You're asking me to go to church? I can't remember the last time I went to church. No. I won't go. Leave me alone, child."

But Mary did not want to give up. She begged him to go with her to church. "Oh, Daddy, if you would only go, God might convert you, and you would be a happy man."

This made John more angry than ever, and with an oath, he pushed his little daughter roughly away from him. Mary turned away with a sad heart, and started walking back to the village. But after a short distance she stopped. "I cannot give up so easily," she said to herself. "I must go back and speak to him again."

Mary's pleadings had affected John more than she knew. Not only was he touched by her obvious love, but he truly was unhappy and yearned to find happiness. When Mary, much to John's surprise, entered the barn again, she began to plead with her father again. He seemed to ignore her, but his heart was being softened by the power of the Holy Spirit.

All at once, John put down his tools and took Mary's hand. "Alright, Mary. I'll go with you to church." His voice was gruff, but Mary didn't mind. He was going with her!

John and Mary went to the house, and after a quick supper they headed toward the village. Quietly, they took a seat in the little church. It seemed as if God had sent a special message to John Linn that evening by the mouth of the preacher, and he listened as if he were the only person present. Afterward, John spoke with the minister, and asked him, between sobs, to pray for him, that his poor soul might not be lost forever.

The minister stayed with John until late in the evening. Now, like Paul, his first question was, "Lord, what wilt thou have me to do?" (Acts 9:6). When he left, John had become a humble man whose only hope was in the righteousness of the Lord Jesus Christ.

For many years John Linn labored especially for the conversion of drunkards, and wherever he went, he spoke about the Lord Jesus Christ who is able to save the chief of sinners.

Question: What is our only hope as sinners?
Scripture readings: Acts 5:20-21, 18:9, 22:14-15, Matthew 10:32.

22. The French Soldier

Henry Durant worked for the French Bible Society. He sold Bibles wherever he could. A regiment of French soldiers was stationed at a nearby army base. Henry was very concerned for the souls of the many soldiers who were ready to be sent into battle.

One day Henry visited the base and asked to see Colonel Thomas, the commanding officer. “Sir,” Henry said after being admitted to the colonel’s office, “I know there is danger that our soldiers will shortly be sent out to fight. May I be given a pass to visit them? I wish to offer them words of encouragement and the Bibles I am selling.”

“You certainly may,” replied the officer. “I expect that we will be called into battle very soon. It would be good if the soldiers had a Bible to take with them.”

With this permission, Henry began to spend as much time as he could talking to the restless soldiers. As he spoke to one group about their need to be saved, he also offered to sell them each a Bible. One strong young man, who had listened carefully, stepped forward and said, “I really believe that what you say is true. I would love to buy a Bible for myself, but I don't have so much as a penny to pay for it."

Henry was deeply touched by the young man's interest. "Why, sir!" he responded, "if you are sincere, then you shall certainly have a Bible! I will pay for it myself." Henry immediately handed the soldier a Bible. But he was surprised when the soldier began to laugh at him.

"Hah, it worked! I knew I could fool you," the soldier laughed. "And it was very easy, too!"

It took a moment for Henry to recover from the shock. He had thought the soldier was sincere. Now he saw that he was wrong. Speaking firmly he said, "Then please give the book back to me."

"Never!" the soldier sneered. "You gave it to me and I plan to keep it. I can use the pages for cigarette paper!"

As the soldier turned away with another mocking laugh, Henry called after him, "Be careful what you do with God's Word. It is a fearful thing to fall into the hands of the living God." (Hebrews 10:31)

Henry left the mocking group. He felt sad and discouraged. Returning to his room, he fell on his knees and earnestly prayed, "Oh Lord, please forgive the mocking soldier and use the stolen Bible for his conversion."

Only a few days later the soldiers sailed out to join in a fierce battle. But Ben, the mocking soldier, remained careless and tore page after page from his Bible. Other soldiers laughed each time, remembering how cleverly he had fooled the missionary. After sailing for several days, Ben was told that they would be joining the battle the following day. Their ship would be in the most dangerous position. This news sent a wave of fear through him. He began to have serious thoughts for the first time. Suddenly the missionary's words flashed through his mind: "It is a fearful thing to fall into the hands of the living God." (Hebrews 10:31)

Ben could not sleep that night, but tossed and turned. He was filled with awful fear. He could only think of the approaching danger and a righteous God. "What if something happens tomorrow and I do fall into God's hands!" He shuddered. His wicked life passed before him. If only he could live his life over.

As soon as the first light of dawn filtered in, Ben got his Bible from his trunk. He was almost too afraid to read it. He expected to see himself condemned on every page. But fear drove him to open the ragged Bible. The words that met his eye were a great surprise for him. "God sent not His Son into the world to condemn the world; but that the world through Him might be saved." (John 3:17) Encouraged, he turned the pages to read more. "He that hath the Son hath life." (1 John 5:12) Thoughtfully he read further, "Come unto me, all ye that labor and are heavy laden, and I will give you rest." (Matthew 11:28) These words deeply impressed him. But while he was still thinking about what he had read, the call to action sounded.

Ben entered into the battle together with the other soldiers on board. The fighting was heavy, and many lives were lost. Suddenly Ben was struck in his chest by a bullet. As soon as they reached land again, he was brought to the hospital; he was seriously wounded. For several weeks Ben was very ill. But while the fever raged, the Spirit of God was working in his heart. The more Ben saw how sinful he was, the more he realized that he needed the Savior. Only the blood of Jesus could wash away his sin.

Ben was still very ill when he was sent back to his own home. Everyone could see that he had come home to die. But they could also see that Ben was a changed man. He was always reading from his tattered Bible. He was always begging his mother and friends to listen to the voice of God in His Word. He tried to tell them how terrible it would be if they would fall into the hands of the living God. After six weeks, Ben died, but not without faith and hope. He had received grace to trust in the Lord and Savior, Jesus Christ.

Henry, the missionary, had not forgotten the careless soldier. He had often prayed for him, begging the Lord to remember him in mercy. One day he returned to the same town where he had met the soldiers. He saw that a funeral was taking place. That evening

Henry was in a restaurant for his evening meal. He noticed that something was different. The waitresses were usually noisy, smiling as they served. But now they were very sad and quiet as they did their work. Henry noticed the owner bent over her work at the counter. He walked over to her and said, "Good evening, Mrs. Pierre." When the woman looked up, he saw tears streaming down her face. "What has happened that makes you so sad?" Henry asked.

"Oh, sir!" she sobbed. "My dear son was buried today. He was a soldier who was sent into battle a couple of months ago. He was seriously wounded and was brought home to die."

"I'm very sorry to hear that; please accept my sympathy," Henry said. "There is no way that I can comfort you. But I have a Book that is the only source of real comfort." Henry opened his Bible and said, "Listen to what it says." With that he began to read to her from a comforting chapter.

As Henry continued reading, he did not see the shocked expression on Mrs. Pierre's face when she saw his Bible. After a few moments, she interrupted his reading. 'Wait!" she exclaimed, "I have something to show you!" She hurried from the room and soon returned with Ben's shabby Bible. "Look!" she said. "This is what my son gave me before he died. It was his most precious possession. This book looks exactly like yours!"

Henry took the book and wondered why it was so badly torn. Opening the cover he saw something the soldier had written: "Received from a missionary on June 25. First used for cigarette paper, but later read, believed, and used by the Lord to save my soul. Benjamin Pierre."

Immediately Henry remembered the day he had spoken with the mocking soldiers. He especially remembered the soldier who had tricked him, the one for whom he had continued to pray. Those mocking words had continued to ring in his ears. Now as Henry listened to Mrs. Pierre's story, he was astonished. His heart was lifted in praise and thanksgiving to the Lord who had heard and answered his prayers.

Henry remembered the warning he had called out to the soldier. He remembered how discouraged he had often been since that time. He had felt that all his work was in vain. Now he saw that the Holy Spirit had used that final warning to the conversion of this young soldier. With a thankful heart, Henry continued his missionary labors with new courage.

Question: What did Ben receive before he died? How does this story encourage us to persevere in doing the Lord's work, even when others mock us?
Scripture reading: Isaiah 55.

23. The Lord Delivers His Own

Henry and Gerrit were very good friends. For many years they did everything together. Much of what they did was not good. Neither Henry nor Gerrit had learned that they needed a Savior. Their parents had never told them about the Lord. They had never taught the boys to respect and honor God's people. They never went to church on Sunday. In fact, Henry and Gerrit hated the Lord's people. They always tried to find ways to cause trouble for them.

Old Mr. Talbo lived in their village. He was a God-fearing man and always attended church faithfully. Mr. Talbo lived alone, even though he had become an old man. Henry really hated Mr. Talbo. Every time he passed by the old man's house, he tried to think of ways to harm him.

One evening Henry approached Mr. Talbo's house. He saw Mr. Talbo sitting inside by his window reading the Bible. Henry could not stand to see the reverence for God's Word reflected in the face of the old man. Hatred boiled up inside of him and he decided to put an end to the old man's peace.

Henry waited until it began to get dark. Then he crept up to the door near where Mr. Talbo sat. Softly he opened the door and crouched down quietly just inside. He hoped he could attack the old man without being seen. Mr. Talbo saw someone coming, but before he realized what was happening, he saw someone leap toward him. Suddenly he felt pain shoot through his head and back as this person began hitting him.

Mr. Talbo recognized his attacker and cried out, "Henry, stop! Oh, Henry! Why are you hitting me?"

Henry was shocked to hear his name from the old man's lips. But Mr. Talbo's next words entered into his heart like an arrow. "You may kill me if you want, Henry. But God will bring you into judgment for this!"

The Lord used these words to show Henry how sinful he was. He saw what a terrible thing he had just done. He saw what a wicked life he had been living. Henry was filled with fear. How could God let such a terrible sinner live for another minute? He expected to die and appear before the judgment seat of God immediately! With a heartfelt cry, Henry ran from Mr. Talbo's house. Once outside, he cried out, "Oh Lord, have mercy on me!" Henry became like Paul in the Bible, one whom the Lord stopped in the middle of his wickedness.

This experience led to Henry's conversion. His friends no longer cared for him. 'Why

Henry!" they mocked, "what's wrong with you? Are you too good for us now?" Henry tried to tell them that they, too, needed to be converted.

Soon Henry was left alone. But after several months, Gerrit came to see him again. The two friends were now very different in their thinking. But they would still go for long walks up the mountains. Henry tried to tell Gerrit how lost people were without the Lord and how wonderful God was for His people. But Gerrit was not interested in what Henry had to say.

One day Henry and Gerrit went for a longer walk than usual. Henry was telling Gerrit about the providence of God—how God takes care of everything that He has created. "Gerrit," Henry explained, "the Bible tells us that the Lord even looks after the sparrows. Not even one of them can fall to the ground unless it is His will. Why, it even says that He knows exactly how many hairs you have on your head!" (Matthew 10:29-30)

"I don't believe you," Gerrit replied. "I don't even believe that the Bible is God's Word. You just want me to believe that as an excuse for being so different lately."

"But it is true! It is also true that you need a new heart. You must be saved before you die or eternity will be terrible for you." Henry tried to help his friend understand, but Gerrit would not listen.

"Let's talk about something else now, Henry. I'm tired of listening to your stories."

Just as Gerrit finished speaking, the boys heard a terrible noise from high up the mountain. Both boys looked up and were instantly filled with terror. A huge snowslide was coming down the mountain straight towards them! The slide was taking everything in its path. Huge trees were snapped off, and wild animals were running frantically, trying to escape. But neither of them could run fast enough. The wall of snow covered everything in sight.

Desperately Henry looked around. There was no time, and no place, to which they could run. He grabbed Gerrit's arm and pulled him behind the nearest tree. "Henry, this tree can't save us!" Gerrit shouted. "Look at those huge trees being crushed!"

"But God can save us! Pray, Gerrit! Pray!'

Even as Henry finished speaking, the snowslide reached them with all its power. But a wonderful thing happened. Their tree became the dividing line for the awful slide. The boys watched in amazement as the wall of snow rushed past them on both sides! Soon everything was deathly silent as they looked at the path of destruction left behind.

Both boys fell on their knees. Henry prayed aloud, "Oh Lord! We thank Thee for saving our lives. We thank Thee for caring for us in Thy great providence."

As the two boys made their way back home, Gerrit was very quiet. Finally he said,

"I believe what you told me, Henry. Only God could save us today. Now I see that there is a God. I have sinned against Him greatly."

The Lord used this wonderful deliverance to stop Gerrit in his sins. Now he could understand the change in Henry. The Lord continued His work in Gerrit's life and later called him to serve as a minister. For many years, Gerrit preached the Word of God in many of the towns in the mountains of his home country.

Question: What does the providence of God mean?
Scripture reading: Psalm 121.

24. The Old Colonel

One cold winter evening, a tall, ragged man wandered into the Water Street Chapel in the heart of New York City to warm himself. This man was known as "the old colonel."

He was over sixty years old, but looked older. He had a long, dirty, gray beard. His gray hair was filthy and uncut, hanging way down his back. His eyes were red. His face was rugged and dirty. His ragged overcoat was fastened with a nail. His pants were filled with holes. Instead of shoes, he had rags, tied with strings, on his feet.

Sin and whiskey had brought the old colonel to this pitiable condition. One would never have thought that he was a college graduate, that he had studied law in the office of President Lincoln's great law secretary, Stanton!

Seeing the lights on in the small chapel, "the old colonel" stepped inside to warm himself for a few minutes. A visiting minister was preaching that evening and the truth of God's Word struck "the old colonel." His entire life of sin became real. In the middle of the service he cried out, "Oh God, if it is not too late, forgive this old sinner!"

Every time the church was open, "the old colonel" was now there. No one paid closer attention to the Word being preached than he. From that moment on he was a changed man, both inwardly and outwardly. Later, when the Lord revealed Himself as a complete Savior for completely lost sinners, there was not a more joyous and thankful person in the church than "the old colonel." He told everyone, his former slum-area friends and his new church friends, that Jesus came to save sinners, of whom he was the chief.

He often looked back in amazement upon the time that he was directed to step into the little chapel on Water Street. He often testified that God's grace in saving such an old, established, backslidden sinner as he, was too great for him to understand; yet, he knew that it was true.

Question: In Mark 5:1-20, who did God change inwardly and outwardly?
Scripture reading: 2 Chronicles 33:1-20.

25. The Widow's Son

A God-fearing widow had only one son. She had taught him from the Bible and prayed with him since he was a child. But he caused her much sadness for he grew up to be a disobedient boy. He laughed at her warnings and tears. Yet she continued to pray for him.

As he grew older, he went from bad to worse. Finally, he fell into the hands of a judge. As was the custom then, he was whipped, branded with a red-hot iron, and put in prison. Still his mother continued to pray for him. At last, he was freed and signed up for service on a ship where no one would know him. He lived a very rough life at sea and then one day, a terrible storm smashed the ship against some rocks, killing all the other crew men except for him. Covered with wounds, he landed on the shore of an island.

Some heathen natives found him and locked him in a hut. Each year they chose the best-looking person on the island to kill as an offering to their sea-god idol. They thought this "white man" was the best offering they could ever give. The young man was sure to die a terrible death.

Suddenly great fear came upon the natives. They saw the scars on his chest and back. They could not give a blemished offering! They had to set the young man free. Finding shelter in a coconut tree, he eventually managed to signal to a passing ship which was sailing to his native land. The captain gave him a place in the bottom of the ship and forgot about him.

Left in this lonely place, the Holy Spirit made him think deeply. He remembered the dangers which God had brought him through. He remembered his mother's warnings, tears, and prayers. God now chose to answer her prayers and the young man was converted. An old seaman gave him a Bible and he read chapter after chapter as one who is hungry and thirsty. The Holy Spirit blessed what he read to his heart. Out of his deep misery he cried, "Show mercy to me, oh God! Show mercy to me, a great sinner! Oh hear my prayer!" He was driven to the Lord Jesus and His atoning blood and found peace. Oh, if only his mother were still living! If only she could know that her prayers were now answered!

Question: When conversion is true in a person's life, how will his life be different from what it was before? In 3 John 4 what is the joy of the writer?
Scripture reading: Galatians 5:19-26.

26. Tom Pays the Price

Reverend McPhail lived in Scotland near Fort George. Many British soldiers were stationed there. This fort was located on the edge of the Moray Firth. It was necessary to take a ferry in order to reach the town on the other side of the firth. Close to Fort George was a small market with several small stores.

One day, as Reverend McPhail was waiting for the ferry, a soldier walked past and stopped at a nearby meat shop. He watched as the soldier paced back and forth comparing prices. At last the soldier picked up a large sausage and handing it to the butcher, asked, "How much for this sausage?"

"This sausage is $2.50 per pound," replied the butcher as he placed it on the scale, "so for two pounds it comes to $5.00."

"What!" exclaimed the soldier, "I'll never pay such a price for that sausage!" He followed his outburst with a terrible oath in which he called on God to damn his soul if he paid the five dollars to the butcher.

"Well, sir," the butcher answered calmly, "that is the price. Do you want it or not?"

The soldier continued to argue for some time, but finally he agreed to pay the butcher's price and bought the sausage.

Reverend McPhail stood in shocked silence as he listened to the soldier's awful words. Watching the soldier make his way down the street, Reverend McPhail decided that he had to find an opportunity to speak to him.

Casually catching up with the soldier, Reverend McPhail fell in step with him and remarked, "What a beautiful day we are having today!"

"Yes, it certainly is," answered the soldier.

"Are you are stationed here at Fort George?"

"Yes, and what a boring place it is! All we ever do is drill, drill, drill."

"I can hear from your accent that you are from England. What is your name?"

"My name's Tom Dunstad," the soldier replied warily.

"Say, that looks like a good sausage you have there," continued Rev. McPhail.

"And it was cheap, too!" boasted Tom.

"What did you pay for it?"

"Why it was only five dollars and just look at the size of it! It's two whole pounds!"

Reverend McPhail was quiet for a moment. Then looking seriously at the young soldier he said, "My friend, you paid a much higher price than that."

Tom looked at him in surprise. "No way!" he exclaimed, "I paid five dollars for it, and not a penny more. I bought it from the butcher over there. If you don't believe me, just ask him."

"I know that's what you think," Reverend McPhail continued, "but you also gave your very soul for that sausage. I heard your oath in which you called upon God to damn your soul if you would pay five dollars for that sausage! Yet in the end you did pay exactly five dollars for it. And now, what is to become of you?"

But just as he said this, Reverend McPhail looked up to see his ferry loading at the dock, so he quickly said "good-bye" to the soldier and hurried on board the ferry.

Tom stood open-mouthed as he watched Reverend McPhail hurry away. Then he returned to the Fort. Tossing his cap on a bench, he sat down. The stranger's words had struck him. He sat with his head down, with those words ringing in his ears. "You gave your very soul for that sausage. And now, what is to become of you?"

Tom tried to shrug off the stranger's words, but they sounded like a death sentence in his ears. He had never before stopped to think about the seriousness of speaking words that he thought sounded tough. For the first time, Tom saw the reality of his lost condition for eternity. He felt as though he stood exposed before the justice of God. "What is to become of you?" sounded over and over in his mind. Terror rose in his heart as he began to pace back and forth. At last he rushed from the Fort and arrived, out of breath, at the ferry dock. Seeing a dock worker, he shouted, "Where is the man in black clothes who was just here? Where did he go?"

"Oh, you mean the minister? He went across on the ferry just half an hour ago."

Despair swept over Tom like a rising tide. But looking up, he saw another ferry just coming in. As soon as he was able, he boarded the ferry and waited impatiently until they reached the opposite shore. After arriving, he asked several of the dock hands if they knew where the minister lived.

After receiving directions, he started out finding that he had to walk several hours across a moor, a deserted stretch of wasteland. Towards evening, Tom arrived at a small village and soon found his way to Reverend McPhail's house. His knock was answered immediately by Reverend McPhail himself. Tom was warmly received and soon told him how his words had struck terror into his heart. "Please tell me what to do!" he exclaimed with tears running down his face. "We may be going into battle soon, and I see eternity before my eyes! Oh, I shall be lost, lost, lost!"

Reverend McPhail rejoiced inwardly to hear the concern that was stirred in the heart of the young man before him. Late into the night he instructed Tom in the way of salvation. Tom stayed for two more days, and the Lord blessed this instruction to his soul.

Tom returned to Fort George a changed man. He returned to the butcher and asked forgiveness for the terrible way in which he had spoken to him. Tom also warned his fellow soldiers about their carelessness concerning their own souls. Over time he saw more and more how gracious God had been to him in arresting him by the words of a stranger. Tom began to attend services at the army chapel where he received precious instruction. The Lord showed him that for him too there was deliverance. Tom learned to sing many of the sacred songs used in the services. He could often be heard singing what became his favorite song:

He took me out of the pit
And from the miry clay;
He set my feet on the Rock
Establishing my way;
He put a song in my mouth
My God to glorify:
And He'll take me some day
To my home on high.

Question: Why is your soul precious?
Scripture reading: Psalm 40.

Prayer points

Missionary Tales

1. ★ Thank God for the power of His Word. Pray for new Christians who read it. Ask God to help them and you to understand and obey.
⌘ Ask God to help you submit to Him. Ask Him to teach your heart as well as your head.

2. ★ Thank Jesus for His love to those who have rejected Him. Ask Him to help you show His love to others.
⌘ Ask God to touch your heart and break your proud nature. Ask Him for the desire to repent of your sins.

3. ★Ask God to make you a good example to others and to those who have no regard for God and His Word. Thank the Lord for changing you and pray that He would increasingly make you like His Son.
⌘ Ask Him to humble your heart so that you are willing to obey and believe in Him.

4. ★Ask God to keep you safe from harm. Pray for the millions of orphans in Africa whose parents have died as a result of war and disease and who have not yet heard the gospel.
⌘ Ask God to forgive your sin of rejecting the truth you have been blessed to hear.

5. ★Ask God to help you grow as a Christian and to grow more and more tender in His Word.
⌘ Ask God to show you your sin and to make you sorry for it. Ask Him for a clean heart.

6. ★Pray for missionaries in other countries. Ask God to help them with any homesickness.
⌘ Ask God to make you long to listen to His Word that is preached.

7. ★Pray for medical missionaries. Pray that the patients will trust in Jesus Christ and that God will bless the medical and spiritual work.
⌘ Pray that you will realize that without Jesus your soul is spiritually sick and deserves eternal damnation, but that with Him you will receive eternal life.

8. ★Ask God to keep you safe spiritually and physically and to help you to be fair and just to all people.
⌘ Ask God to convict you of your sin when you are mean to other people. Ask Him to show you that you need Christ as does everyone in the world.

9. ★Thank God for listening to and answering prayers. Praise Him for His power over the universe. Thank Him for doing all things right.
⌘ Ask Christ to show you that He is the only way to the Father and the only One who can give us eternal life and save us from hell.

10. ★Ask God to protect you and your family from danger. Thank Him for all the times He has protected you in the past, even when you didn't realize you were in danger.
⌘ Pray that God will show you your desperate need of salvation and forgive you for all the times you have heard His Word and haven't trusted in Him. Ask Him to give you a new heart.

Remarkable Conversions

11. ★Ask God to give you the right words to say when people ask you questions about the gospel.
    ⌘ Pray that you will trust in Jesus Christ alone and in His death on the Cross as your only and sufficient hope for salvation.

12. ★Ask God to protect you from sin and temptation. Pray that your family and friends will come to know Christ and that God will use you to bring His Word to their attention.
    ⌘ Pray that you will call upon the Lord while He is near and believe in the Lord Jesus Christ while you are still young.

13. ★Pray for missions that reach out to prisoners. Pray that Christians in prison will be able to stand up for God in a difficult environment.
    ⌘ Ask God to show you how you too are a prisoner if you do not trust in Christ. Ask God to stop the control that sin has over you.

14. ★Pray for your church leaders. Ask God to strengthen them and provide for them. Ask Him to protect them and their families.
    ⌘ Pray that you will trust in Christ to provide you with salvation and keep you from a hardened heart.

15. ★Ask God to show you what His will is for your life. Pray for those who God has called to be preachers and pastors. Ask God to make them obedient to His call and His Word.
    ⌘ Ask God to make you listen and obey the warnings in His Word and to turn from sin and give your life to God to use as He wishes.

16. ★Thank God for looking after you even when you didn't ask Him to. Thank Him for His love even when you hated Him.
⌘ Ask God to give you His love in your heart. Repent of those times when you were angry at Him and His Word instead of being obedient.

17. ★Pray that God will remind you of His Word when you are tempted to sin. Thank Him for the good influence of the Christians you know.
⌘ Pray that God will teach you that there is no hope without Jesus Christ. Ask Him to convince you that those who hear His Word will be accountable for it.

18. ★Thank God for His power over sin. Ask Him to deliver you from temptation and from making the same mistakes.
⌘ Ask God to forgive your sins. Ask Him to make you sorry when you disobey Him.

19. ★Thank God for the reality of heaven and that one day His people will be there with Him.
⌘ Pray that God will teach you the seriousness of eternity without Him. Ask Him to make you sorry for your sins, not just their consequences.

20. ★Thank God for forgiving you so that you are free to love Him. Ask Him to help you to love Him more.
⌘ Thank God for His faithfulness and love. Thank Him that He still is presenting you with His Word. Turn to Him and ask forgiveness for your sins. Ask Him to give you a real love for Him in your heart.

21. ★Ask God to show you what He wants you to do. Ask Him to soften your heart so that you are willing to obey Him.
⌘ Ask God to soften your heart so that you will listen to His words of mercy and love in Christ Jesus.

22. ★Pray for those who are preaching God's Word. Pray for specific people you know who are rejecting Him.
⌘ Ask God to help you listen to and obey His Word when it is brought to you by people who love and trust Him.

23. ★Thank God for His detailed care of you in so many ways.
⌘ Repent of the many times you have gone through a day forgetting about God and living without Him.

24. ★Thank God that there is no one too old or too young for Him to save.
⌘ Ask God to convict you of your sin. Ask Him to deliver you from falling into sin and temptation in the future.

25. ★Ask God to protect you from taking His name in vain. Praise Him for how wonderful and loving He is.
⌘ Ask God to change your heart and to keep you from forgetting the truths you have learned.

26. ★Thank the Lord for giving you salvation and for the joy that is in your heart. Ask Him to put a watch over your lips.
⌘ Ask the Lord to deliver you from the trap of sin and to give you His salvation. Ask for a heart that is open to His Word.

Scripture Index for Book 2

1. Acts 8:26-40

2. 1 Corinthians 9:16-23

3. Matthew 5:38-48

4. Acts 14:1-18

5. 1 Kings 18:20-40
   Habakkuk 2:18-20
   1 Corinthians 8:4-6

6. John 14:1-3
   Colossians 3:23-24
   Revelation 21:1-6

7. Luke 2:10-11
   1 Corinthians 2:6-16

8. 2 Samuel 9
   Matthew 7:12

9. Psalm 34:17; Psalm 34

10. Psalm 91; Psalm 91:3 Psalm 91:4
    2 Timothy 4:18
    2 Peter 2:9

11. John 14:6
    Acts 10:6

12. Proverbs 23:32
    Ecclesiastes 11:1
    Zechariah 3:2

13. Luke 23:39-43

14. Matthew 4:18-22
    Mark 1:16-18

15. Mark 5:1-20
    1 Corinthians 15:56-57
    1 Timothy 1:15

16. Psalm 107:30
    Matthew 6:33
    Acts 26:12-32
    2 Corinthians 5:17
    1 Timothy 1:13
    1 Peter 2:9

17. Psalm 107:17-32
    Isaiah 57:20-21
    Haggai 1: 12&13
    Luke 12:48

18. Psalm 51
    Nahum 1:7

19. Psalm 34:11-22
    Habakkuk 3:2

20. Hosea 14
    Luke15:11-32

21. Matthew 10:32
    Acts 5:20-21, 9:6, 18:9, 22:14-15

22. Isaiah 55
    Matthew 11:28
    John 3:17
    Hebrews 10:31
    1 John 5:12

23. Psalm 121
    Matthew 10:29-30

24. Mark 5:1-20
    2 Chronicles 33:1-20

25. Galatians 5:19-26
    3 John 4

26. Psalm 40

Answers

1. That he was a sinner and that Christ is the only Savior for sinners.
2. Discuss.
3. Her conduct - when she didn't lose her temper.
4. Food and love.
   To read the Bible.
   She is praying for the people in her village to be freed from superstition and realise their need of Christ.
5. One.
   Idols are lies. They cannot speak. There is no life in them.
6. Heaven, with Christ.
   The Lord will give a reward.
7. It is dead.
8. They were both unsaved sinners.
   They both loved the Lord Jesus Christ.
9. They prayed to God and he saved them from the pirates.
10. God allowed him to oversleep so that he couldn't visit the chief who was planning to kill him. His escape led to the Chief's conversion.
11. Jesus Christ.
    The Holy Spirit.
12. A serpent or an adder.
    God answered the prayers of his mother after "many days."
13. Mercy.
    He found a job, married a God-fearing woman, served the Lord, and evangelized his friends.

14. Discuss.
    They teach us about God, sin and salvation, striving to catch sinners in the gospel net of God's salvation in Jesus Christ.
15. A sinful heart.
16. Blasphemers and persecutors.
17. One who has heard about Christ and still has not believed.
    I am with you.
18. The Spirit of God.
    That God is good; a stronghold in the day of trouble and that He knoweth them that trust in Him.
19. Discuss (We have sinful natures; we are weak).
    Habakkuk asks God to remember mercy.
20. Discuss backsliding.
21. The righteousness of the Lord Jesus Christ.
22. Grace to trust in the Lord Jesus Christ.
    God can use our words to convert someone long after we have spoken.
23. God takes care of everything.
24. The demon possessed man.
25. Discuss.
    They desire to obey God, their chief end in life will be to glorify God.

    He has no greater joy than to hear that His children walk in the truth.
26. It is given to you by God; it is eternal; your soul will spend eternity in one of two places - heaven or hell. Heaven is eternal life; hell is eternal death.

Classic Devotions by F.L. Mortimer

Use these books alongside an open Bible and you will learn more about characters such as Cain and Abel, Abraham, Moses and Joshua, amongst others. You will enjoy the discussion generated and the time devoted to devotions and getting into God's Word. Investigate the Scriptures and build your knowledge with question and answer sessions with F. L. Mortimer's range of classic material. Written over a hundred years ago, this material has been updated to include activities and discussion starters for today's family.

ISBN: 1-85792-5866
1-85792-5858
1-85792-5912

Mary Jones and her Bible

a true life story
a classic favorite

The traditional story of the young Welsh girl who treasured God's Word and struggled for many years to get a copy of her own. An excellent reminder of our Christian heritage. ISBN:1-85792-5688

Other books published by Christian Focus Publications in connection with Reformation Heritage Books.

Bible Questions and Answers
by Carine Mackenzie
and *Teachers' Manual* by Diana Kleyn.

ISBN 1-85792-702-8
1-85792-701-4

Doctrines and subjects covered in these two titles include:

God

Creation

How man sinned

What happened because of sin

Salvation

Jesus as Prophet, Priest, and King

The Ten Commandments

Keeping God's Laws

The way to be saved

Experiencing God's salvation

Baptism and the Lord's Supper

Prayer

Where is Jesus now?

Death

Hell

Heaven

Building on the Rock
Books 1-5

If you enjoyed this book:

Book 2
How God Stopped the Pirates
Missionary Tales and
Remarkable Conversions

You will also enjoy the others in this series by Joel R. Beeke and Diana Kleyn

Book 1
How God Used a Thunderstorm

Living for God and The Value of Scripture

Book 3
How God Used a Snowdrift

Honoring God and

Dramatic Rescues

Book 4
How God Used a Drought and an Umbrella

Faithful Witnesses and

Childhood Faith

Book 5
How God Sent a Dog to Save a Family

God's Care and

Childhood Faith

The Complete Classic Range: Worth Collecting

A Basket of Flowers
1-85792-5254

Christie's Old Organ
1-85792-5238

A Peep Behind the Scenes
1-85792-5254

Little Faith
1-85792-567X

Childhood's Years
1-85792-713-3

Saved at Sea
1-85792-795-8

Children's Stories
by D L Moody
1-85792-640-4

Mary Jones and Her Bible
1-85792-5688

Children's Stories by J C Ryle
1-85792-639-0

Trailblazers

Real life stories of people who made a difference!

Corrie ten Boom, The Watchmaker's Daughter ISBN 1 85792 116X
Joni Eareckson Tada, Swimming against the Tide
ISBN 1 85792 833 4
Adoniram Judson, Danger on the Streets of Gold
ISBN 1 85792 6609
Isobel Kuhn, Lights in Lisuland
ISBN 1 85792 6102
C.S. Lewis, The Story Teller
ISBN 1 85792 4878
Martyn Lloyd-Jones, From Wales to Westminster
ISBN 1 85792 3499
George Müller, The Children's Champion
ISBN 1 85792 5491
John Newton, A Slave Set Free NEW
ISBN 1 85792 834 2
John Paton, A South Sea Island Rescue
ISBN 1 85792 852 0
Mary Slessor, Servant to the Slave
ISBN 1 85792 3480
Hudson Taylor, An Adventure Begins
ISBN 1 85792 4231
William Wilberforce, The Freedom Fighter
ISBN 1 85792 3715
Richard Wurmbrand, A Voice in the Dark
ISBN 1 85792 2980
Gladys Aylward, No Mountain Too High
ISBN 1 85792 5947

Bible Stories and Non Fiction

Bible Time, Bible Wise, Bible Alive and The Bible Explorer

All by Carine Mackenzie.

The Bible Explorer: 1-85792-5335